McGee & Me!
The Not-So-Great Escape: Three Books in One

Look for other exciting McGee and Me! products from
Tyndale House Publishers!

McGee and Me! Videos
>   #1 The Big Lie
>   #2 A Star in the Breaking
>   #3 The Not-So-Great Escape
>   #4 Skate Expectations
>   #5 Twister & Shout
>   #6 Back to the Drawing Board
>   #7 Do the Bright Thing
>   #8 Take Me Out of the Ball Game
>   #9 'Twas the Night before Christmas

Coming Spring 2000
>   #10 In the Nick of Time
>   #11 The Blunder Years
>   #12 Beauty in the Least

McGee and Me! New Media Kids Bible CD-Rom

McGee and Me! Sticky Situations Game
You can find Tyndale products at fine bookstores everywhere. If you are unable to find any of these products at
your local bookstore, you may write for ordering information to:

> Tyndale House Publishers, Inc.
> Order Services
> P.O. Box 80
> Wheaton, IL 60189

Focus on the Family® presents

The Not-So-
Great Escape

Do the Bright Thing
'Twas the Fight before Christmas

Tyndale House Publishers, Inc.
WHEATON, ILLINOIS

Visit our exciting Web site at www.tyndale.com

McGee & Me! *The Not-So-Great Escape: Three Books in One*

Bill Myers is represented by the literary agency of Alive Communications, Inc.,
1465 Kelly Johnson Blvd., Suite 320, Colorado Springs, CO 80920.

ISBN 0-8423-3665-6

Printed in the United States of America

07	06	05	04	03	02	01	00
7	6	5	4	3	2	1	

CONTENTS

The Not-So-Great Escape

by Bill Myers and Ken C. Johnson

Fix your thoughts on what is true and good and right. Think about things that are pure and lovely, and dwell on the fine, good things in others. (Philippians 4:8, *The Living Bible*)

ONE
The Space Creeper Strikes Again

*Thirty-two right, fourteen left, seventeen right, and finally
nothing left . . . to do but wait, that is. Then slowly the lock on
the door of my lunar prison cell began to open. I stood there,
gripped with suspense. The hefty door swung wide, revealing
what I'd worked on for these many months—my freedom.
Though it had taken only a few moments and some brain
bending calculations to program the lunar lock and figure out
its combination, it had seemed like days. OK, so it had been
days: 136 days to be exact. But, hey, who's counting? I never
really was that good in math anyway.*

*I was counting on one thing, though: Getting out of there!
There had never been a prison in the star system that could
hold the sinister Space Villain for long. Besides, I needed a
change of scenery. Between choking down the galactic glob
they called food and playing several games of "stare down"
with the four walls, this hadn't exactly been a summer vacation. So, with a song in my heart and a sneer on my lips, off
I went.*

*I snaked my way swiftly and quietly down corridor after
darkened corridor. A thousand thoughts raced through my
head: Had I tripped the alarm? Were the android guards on to
me yet? Was my hidden space pod still intact and waiting for*

me in Quadrant Three? Is Colonel Crater's Fried Chicken open this time of night?

Suddenly a phaser blast pierced the darkness. It ricocheted right in front of my feet. As I frantically dodged the blast, I realized one of my questions had been answered: The guards were definitely on to me.

I moved down the corridor, slipping through one hallway and down the other with moves that would make Michael Jackson turn green with nausea . . . uh, envy. The android guards were hot on my trail—this little game of blast attack was getting old fast. If I could just think of something to throw them off track. Maybe get the goons to sit down and swap nut-and-bolt recipes or something. Unfortunately, I had left my Betty Cosmos Cookbook back in my cell. So instead I chose to stick to my original brilliant plan: Run!

Another series of laser bursts grazed past my heels and exploded in front of me. The shots tore a hole in the air vent beside me. Aha! I thought. Their brainless blasting has created an escape route. Amidst a blaze of laserfire I dove for the air duct and squeezed inside. It was just big enough for a notorious space villain of my size.

As I scooted down the shaft I let out a hideous cry to taunt the trigger-happy space droids. "Boooo-ah-ah-ah-ahhh. No one can stop the dastardly Villain, mad master of interplanetary bad guys. No one. Boo-ah-ah-ah!" My eerie laughter echoed down the air shafts, sending chills up the spine of every space guard in the quadrant. (A pretty neat trick considering that all the guards were androids—you know, fancy robots.)

As I worked my way down the air shafts toward my hidden space pod, I recalled how I had gotten into this fix in the first place. I'd been busy doing my usual cosmic crime stuff

throughout fourteen star systems (talk about overworked!):
hijacking Diamel freighters on the planet Zirconia, pillaging
spice mines on the planet Paprika, stealing the sacred singing
stones of Jagger Moon . . . not returning an overdue book from
the public library in Cleveland. Yes, I was an interplanetary
pirate without equal (and without brains, according to the
space cops who'd found my prints all over everything).

Finally the Galactic Governing Council sent out an elite
group of crime fighters, The Blue Fox Squadron. Their leader
was my old rival, Cyborg II. There was even a bounty of
2 million greckles for my capture (about eight bucks in real
money). However, for a goody two-shoes like Cyborg II, the
reward didn't matter. No, not to Mr. Good Guy . . . Mr.
Straight and Narrow . . . Mr. Mom and Asteroid Pie. He did
good deeds just for the sake of doing good deeds—things like
helping little old ladies cross the Forbidden Zone. So it was no
surprise that he would pursue my highly dangerous self across
the universe, risking life and limb for peanuts (unsalted, of
course). After all, he was the hero. It was his job to do that
kind of thing.

My job was to be an evil space villain. Some job. I mean,
the pay and hours were lousy. I was chased night and day,
often had to go without sleep, and usually ran dangerously low
on fuel (and Twinkies). And nobody ever sent me birthday
presents . . . believe me, being a fugitive is a real pain.

Well, one night I fell right into one of Cyborg's clever little
traps. I'd stopped at a safety inspection station—you know,
where they check for faulty thermal reactors, hydro-converters,
and any illegal fruit being taken across the border. When I
eased into the station, a trooper approached my craft. He asked
for my travel code and flight papers, then wanted to know if

5

I was carrying any melons or mangos. When I handed him my papers, he lifted his visor and looked at me with a steely-eyed stare I knew all too well. It was Cyborg II! Faster than you can say, "Obee Won Kenobee," the rest of the Blue Fox Squadron surrounded my ship. Their eyes—and their blasters—were aimed right at me.

There I was, surrounded by fifty of the best crime fighters in the galaxy. Now what? *I thought.* Should I fight to the finish? Create a smoke screen? Try to talk my way out of it?

Then it came to me; it was perhaps the most brilliant scheme I had ever conceived! I slowly lifted my arms into the air. Then through sneering lips I whispered those magic words: "I give up."

You know, sometimes I'm so clever I scare myself.

Next thing I knew I was hauled into space court, yelled at by the space judge, fined seventy-five greckles for the case of melons they found hidden in my trunk, and sentenced to eternity in the Mugsy Moon Rock Institute for the Criminally Clumsy. I'd been there ever since.

Until now, that is. Now I was making my escape. And things were going just as I'd expected them to—rotten.

I ended up crawling around in the stupid air shaft for about an hour trying to find Quadrant Three, where I'd hidden my faithful space pod. No luck. It was still hidden. Then I noticed a flashing light through the grill of a vent up ahead. "Aha! Now we're getting somewhere!" I exclaimed.

Drawing closer, I heard the squawk of a guard droid's two-way radio. I anxiously peered out and saw the mechanical moron pacing back and forth. He obviously had his sensors on the lookout for you-know-who.

Suddenly his radio came alive with an urgent transmission:

"This is Blue Fox Leader. Any sign of escaped villain in Quadrant Five?"

"Negative, Blue Fox," the guard responded. "All quiet here."

"Be on your toes," Blue Fox said. "This villain's a sneaky little character."

"Affirmative, Blue Fox. I've got my eyes peeled and my nose to the ground. Over and out."

Well, that sounded painful, even for an android. But it was also enlightening. Not only was every guard in the compound hot on my trail, but Cyborg II and his Blue Fox boys were close. Real close. That put a knot in my stomach the size of Jupiter. One thing was sure; I didn't spell relief "C-Y-B-O-R-G."

Well, if I was in Quadrant Five, then Quadrant Three was nearby. (I'm great with numbers like that.) However, with a maze of air shafts leading a thousand different directions, Quadrant Three wasn't going to be easy to find. There was one thing that would make that search a little easier, though: the guard's radio. I could use it to pick up on the good guys' chit-chat and maybe avoid an unpleasant encounter or two. Besides, if things got really boring, maybe I could tune in on the Cubs' game.

Great. Now for the hard part—getting the radio away from this bucket of bolts. With my luck, it was probably a Christmas present, and he was going to be all sentimental about it and wanna keep it. Of course, I needed it more than he did. I just had to convince him of that. Right. Unfortunately, he was bigger than I. In fact, he was the biggest android I'd ever seen. He made Hulk Hogan look like Pee Wee Herman. I, on the other hand, made Pee Wee Herman look like King Kong—I think you get the picture.

But I put all my brain power into action and came up with a plan. I'd wait for the droid to pass underneath me, crown him on the noggin' with the air-vent grill, then jump down, scoop up his radio and immobilizer-blaster, and be merrily on my way.

The plan worked great—well, except for a few slight catches. Slight catch number one: my finger. I got it caught in the grill. Since the grill weighed as much as yours truly, you can imagine what happened next. We both came crashing down on top of the guard, knocking the mechanical wonder to the floor.

Than came slight catch number two.

The blow knocked the droid down. What it didn't do was knock him out. I'd forgotten one little thing: Droids are machines—you can't knock a machine out. Soooo, it was like hitting a grizzly bear with a horseshoe—the only thing that gets knocked out is your teeth. As he slowly got up, I knew this could mean some heavy hand-to-hand combat. You know, kung-fu, karate, chop suey.

I decided to take the simplest route. I ran between his legs. I must have really confused his circuits because he started spinning around, trying to see where I'd gone. Every time he turned to find me, I'd run back between his legs. Pretty soon the wires in the droid's neck got wound so tight they snapped. I heard this pop and zing, and he conveniently sank to the ground, a pile of limp metal and fizzling wires.

Ha! And they think I'm brainless.

I scooped up his radio and immobilizer and bounded toward the vent. I chuckled as I crawled up and out of sight. "Assignment Radio Raid" had gone off after all. OK, so it wasn't exactly what you might call a textbook ambush Rambo-style, but it got the job done.

As I continued to trek through the endless air shafts, I occasionally picked up discussions between troopers in certain Quadrant numbers. I was getting closer to finding my space pod—but the radio transmissions showed that Cyborg II was getting closer to finding me, too.

I came to another vent and peered out. There were familiar markings on the wall: Q4S7-Quadrant Four, Sector Seven. All right! One Quadrant away. Soon I'd be neatly tucked into my space pod and blasting off to freedom. "Colonel Crater's Fried Chicken, here I come!"

Suddenly, a familiar voice came blasting across the radio; "Cyborg II, this is Blue Fox Leader. Quadrant Four, Sector Seven is secure. Do you copy?"

Yipes! He was right on top of me!

"Roger, Blue Fox. No sign of Creeper yet," Cyborg II answered.

Just then I heard the haunting sound of footsteps echoing through the corridor below. "Keep your eyes peeled, Cyborg II," I heard someone exclaim.

I peeked through the vent and sure enough, there he was, a guard droid in tow, drawing closer with every step. My fear suddenly vanished. Why should I be afraid? This was perfect. He didn't know I was up here. For once I was the hammer, he was the nail. I was the cat, he was the mouse. I was the little kid, he was the sucker—well, you know what I mean.

Lifting the immobilizer, I drew a bead on the droid. I'd nail him first, then Cyborg II. Oh, I'd just wing them. You know, put them out of commission long enough for my escape. I mean, even we wicked space villains have a little heart.

Cyborg II continued waltzing toward me, unaware of my presence. His crazy droid followed him, glancing around and

9

whistling some old tune. I think it was the theme song from
The Jetsons. *They were getting closer, closer. Cyborg II was in
range now. I placed my finger on the trigger and slowly began
to squeeze . . .*

*Nuts—the rotten guard droid was beginning to sing the
lyrics now. I wondered if the immobilizer had a setting for
"barbecue." I pulled the trigger back. Click . . . click . . . fizz
. . . schweeze . . . Rats! The blaster was out of blast. As
Cyborg II and the droid casually strolled on past, I kept
squeezing the trigger, hoping for the best. If that bucket of
bolts sang much longer, it might kill me. The faulty phaser
just fizzed.*

*"Darned no-account, two-bit blaster," I exclaimed. I tossed
it in disgust as the off-key, metallic rendition of* The Jetsons
trailed off in the distance.

*I sat there pondering my next move. Then another radio
transmission broke the silence: "Blue Fox Leader, this is Cyborg
II. Do you copy?"*

"Go ahead, Cyborg II. I copy."

*"Sir, we've discovered a small space craft in Quadrant
Three, Sector Twelve. I think you ought to check it out."*

"On my way, Cyborg II. Over and out."

*Well, if that wouldn't fry the hair off a wookie. Now, they'd
found my space pod. The one I worked on in space prison
metal shop for months. (I told the guards I was building a
flying toaster.) The one I'd hidden away so carefully so I could
use it to escape. Oh well, I really didn't want to escape
anyway. I was beginning to like it here. Pleasant surroundings.
Courteous staff. Fine dining. Yeah, right.*

*I made a mad dash down the air shaft (as mad a dash
as you can make crawling on bony knees). I crawled so fast,*

I wore holes in the knees of my prison fatigues. Hey, at least I was in style now.

I hoped to reach my space pod in time to spoil Blue Fox's party. I reached the air vent in Quadrant Three and hesitantly took a peek below. I was too late.

Cyborg II was milling about my beloved pod as another Blue Fox trooper came up.

"What is it?" the trooper asked.

"The Creeper's space pod. Set your immobilizers on 'massacre'! We'll destroy the thing before he can put it to use!"

Phasers on 'massacre,' I thought. Gee, I guess they're not kidding around. My only hope was that the pod, made of pure titanium steel, would withstand the phaser blast. If it didn't, I was going to need a lot of duct tape and crazy glue.

The Blue Fox boys began an all-out assault on my tiny space craft. I had to admit I was pleased to see they weren't doing much damage. Their phaser blasts bounced off like tennis balls. Then, just as I decided my ship was going to survive, Cyborg II thew down his blaster in frustration and gave the pod a good swift kick.

Bonk! The little space craft shattered into a million useless little pieces.

"Drat. Lousy, two-bit, no-account titanium," I said. Oh, sure, the stuff can withstand a fifty-megaton explosion. But give it a little punt, and crunch it goes to pieces on you.

Well, I was done for. Clobbered! Slaughtered! Trashed! Kicked! Whipped! Annihilated! Hammered! You get the idea. It didn't matter, though. After all, it was all just in fun.

Oh, didn't I tell you? This while galactic battle was just imagination. Yup! In fact, the whole thing had taken place in my little buddy Nick's front yard, not in the far reaches of outer space.

As for my titanium-covered space pod, well, I guess you could say it was actually a pigskin-covered football. The proton blasters? Harmless little toy guns. The maze of air shafts I've been crawling through . . . well, that was simply the old drain gutter that goes down the side of the house. Even the victorious Cyborg II and Blue Fox boys were none other than Nick and his pal, Louis.

Get the picture?

Now before you get all excited and upset, think it over. A make-believe mission is much better than a real one. No one ever gets hurt, and the clean-up expenses after a battle are almost nil. In fact, there is really only one drawback—getting stuck playing the villain. I mean, basically the villain is a real loser. That's OK, though. Who wants the bad guys to win anyway? Besides, if you play your cards right, even the villain can have a small victory once in a while.

Like thinking up a neat little trick to end the game in your favor.

"A valiant effort, earthling," I said to Nick via the walkie-talkie. "But that was only a three-dimensional projection of my pod."

"McGee, that's not fair!" Nicholas shouted. "We creamed you!"

Nick was right . . . but since when do wicked space villains ever play fair?

"Until we meet again," I called. Then I gave him one final laugh. The famous World's-Most-Wicked-Space-Villain cackle: "Boooo-ah-ah-ah-ahhh!"

Night of the Blood Freaks

"Cheater!" Nicholas shouted into his walkie-talkie.

He hated it when McGee did that. Any time Nick was about to get the upper hand in one of their imaginary games, McGee would suddenly change the rules. Nicholas knew he and Louis had captured the Creeper's space pod fair and square. They'd won! But nooooo. Suddenly the space pod was just a 3-D picture, and Mr. Creeper McGee had disappeared.

It happened all the time, and it always made Nick furious. Oh, well, that was one of the things you had to put up with when a cartoon drawing was your best friend.

Nick and Louis stood over the somewhat flattened football. It had served well as the Creeper's space pod. Now, thanks to their limitless imaginations, it would become something else. Maybe an alien egg about to hatch little alienettes or a space slug about to spew space slime or . . . or . . .

"Nicholas, come on in. It'll be getting dark soon." It was Mom, calling from the front porch.

Nicholas frowned. Moms never understood intergalactic warfare. You could be defending the freedom of the entire galaxy . . . but if it was lunchtime, forget it.

Mutant invaders could be threatening our gene pools . . . but if you forgot to put on your coat before going out, too bad. And if you had homework? Well, you could kiss any superhero activity good-bye. After all, what was more important? Getting an A on a spelling quiz or saving all humanoid life-forms as we know them?

"Oh, Mom . . . ," Nicholas protested.

"Come in—now!"

Suddenly the galaxy's safety didn't seem quite so important. Maybe it was the way she said, "Now!" In any case, Nick knew she meant business. So with a heavy sigh he started toward the porch.

"Getting dark soon?" Louis taunted with a smirk at Nicholas. He loved to tease Nick about his parents. They seemed to have all sorts of rules Nick had to follow—what he could do, what he couldn't do, what music he could listen to, how many hours of TV he could watch. In short, if it was fun, Louis figured Nick's folks had a rule against it.

The boys raced up the stairs and threw open the door to Nicholas's room.

"I don't know, Nick," Louis said with a laugh as he plopped down on the bed. "On TV, Cyborg's mom always makes him come in when it gets dark."

Nick spun around and fired off a good burst of imaginary neutrons from his proton blaster. Fortunately it was still set on "massacre." Louis grabbed his chest and did one of his better dying routines. It was beautiful. He choked, he gasped, he sputtered. Then, just when you thought it was all over, he gave one last twitch. Nick had to grin. It was a brilliant performance. On a scale of one to ten, this was definitely an eleven.

Laughing, Nick took off his helmet, and Louis reached for the newspaper they'd brought from downstairs.

"Hey, check it out," Louis said as he turned to the movie section. *"Night of the Blood Freaks, Part IV* starts tomorrow. And it's in 3-D."

"No kidding?" Nicholas asked. He crossed over to the bed for a better look.

"Remember last year," Louis asked, "in *Twilight of the Blood Freaks* when he got those guys at the campfire?"

"Uh, no," Nicholas said, clearing his throat slightly. "I didn't see it. My folks wouldn't let me."

"Man, they don't let you do anything."

"Hey, that was a year ago," Nick protested. "I'm a lot older now, all right?"

Louis gave a shrug and looked back to the ad in the paper. It was as gory as the title. "Have you seen the commercial?" he asked.

Actually, Nick couldn't have helped but see the commercial. It had been running on TV for the last couple of days. It was really gross and really stupid—which probably meant the film would be a smash.

"Yeah, I've seen it," Nick said.

The two boys looked at each other. Each knew exactly what the other was thinking. (That was one of the neat things about having a close friend.) Slowly, they each took a breath and started speaking, together, "First there was *Dawn of the Blood Freaks* . . . "

They made their voices as deep and ominous as they could. Slowly they rose from the bed and sat on its edge. Their volume began to grow. "Then, *Day of the Blood Freaks.*"

15

They continued, sounding louder and scarier with each word. "Then, *Twilight of the Blood Freaks.*"

They plopped their feet down hard on the floor at exactly the same time. "But now—" slowly they rose to their feet—"as shadows begin to fall it's . . . *Night of the Blood Freaks!*"

They screamed and groaned at the top of their lungs, their bodies bouncing and jerking out of control. One minute it looked like they were doing Frankenstein. The next, some new dance step. Then they grabbed their throats and began to cough and choke—all the time screaming their lungs out.

Meanwhile, several families on both sides of the Martin's home stopped what they were doing. What was that sound? What was going on? A few even stepped out onto their front porch for a better listen. From all the screaming and shouting, it was pretty obvious that someone was either being tortured or murdered. Maybe both.

But a few neighbors didn't pay any attention to the racket. They knew Nicholas. They knew about his imagination.

When Nicholas and his family had first moved into Grandma's house, they were pretty excited. After all, here was a fantastic Victorian house that was over a hundred years old. Who knew what secrets the attic held? Who knew what was under those creaky floorboards in the hallway? Who knew which loose bricks in the basement could be moved to discover a secret passageway?

These were the things they expected. What they didn't expect were drafty rooms in the winter or cold showers in the morning (whenever the hot water heater was on the fritz—which was a lot). Above all, they certainly didn't expect a house without a dishwasher! I mean, this was nearly the twenty-first century, for crying out loud. Surely Grandma would have a dishwasher!

Well, to be honest, Grandma did have a dishwasher. But like everything else in the house it was a "teensy bit on the broken side." And since Dad wasn't famous for being a handyman (well, he was famous—but in the wrong way), they had to wait and bring in a repairman.

Until then, guess whose children got to wash and dry the dishes by hand! Tonight it was Sarah's turn to wash and Nicholas's turn to dry. They had fried chicken with mashed potatoes and gravy. Grandma's favorite. But not Sarah's. It's not that she minded the taste. It was the cleaning up she hated. Especially the gravy. Especially after they let it sit around for half an hour and it had dried into rubbery, crusty gunk. And, as we all know, once gunk dries, it's impossible to scrape off of dishes. Sarah tried—but not without plenty of sighs, whines, and sarcastic comments only a girl going on fourteen can make.

"This is gross," she muttered. "Why do I always get stuck washing on the gunk days?"

She opened the lid to the plastic garbage can and began to chisel at one of the plates. Chicken bones, gravy, and a few hidden green beans bounced and splattered against an empty milk carton.

Whatever, the family dog, was right there, too. Actually, Whatever was mostly Sarah's dog. Nicholas didn't much care for the little fur ball. The critter always seemed to be whining and yapping. Come to think of it, maybe that was why Sarah and Whatever were such good pals—they were so much alike.

Anyway, Whatever was standing off to the side, barking and begging. He always did that when they had chicken. Forget the stewed tomatoes, the liver, the cooked cauliflower. Anytime you'd try to slip a handful of those delicacies under the table to him so your plate looked clean, he was nowhere to be found. Come chicken night, though, you couldn't get rid of the pest.

"Make sure he doesn't get any of those bones," Mom warned Sarah as she headed into the family room.

Sarah sighed—her answer to just about everything these days. She knew Whatever liked to chew the bones. She also knew that chicken bones cracked and splintered and that if Whatever got any and swallowed them, he might really hurt himself.

She knew all this—but she also knew how much he liked chicken.

At first she was able to ignore him—but the persistent little critter kept sitting there whining and begging with the most pitiful look on his face. Of course, Nicholas thought he always looked pitiful. But this time, he was pitifully pitiful.

The dog kept working on Sarah's emotions. He used every trick in the begging handbook. Droopy eyes. Pathetic whines. Sad sighs. Nick thought it was disgusting. Revolting. The fact that it was exactly what he used to do to get his way with his parents never even dawned on him.

Finally, it worked. Sarah gave in.

It wasn't a big piece. Just a chicken wing. And she really didn't "officially" give it to Whatever. She just sort of let it

18

fall on the floor. Then, before she could grab it, he sort of took it and ran off.

Nicholas started to say something (loud enough, of course, for Mom to hear). Then Sarah shot him the old if-you-know-what's-good-for-you-you'll-keep-your-mouth-shut look. Normally that look would be just what Nick needed to make him say something. But having battled the Space Creeper all afternoon, Nick wasn't ready for another fight.

Instead he asked quietly, under his breath, "You sure you want him eating that?"

"Don't sweat it; he loves chicken," she muttered. "One piece isn't going to hurt him. No biggie."

But for Whatever, it was about to become a biggie. A life-and-death biggie . . .

THREE
Grounded

The next morning, *Night of the Blood Freaks* was the talk of the school.

They talked about it on the bus. They talked about it at recess. They talked about it at lunch. The lunch talks were the best. Usually, one of the guys would go into great gory detail over what he expected to see. And usually one of the girls would look down at the ketchup dripping off her hamburger . . . and suddenly lose her appetite.

Later in the day, the kids started drawing pictures and passing them around. Dripping fangs here. Crazed, bloodshot eyes there. Of course, Nick drew the best. That was one thing he could do—draw. He'd never been too much into drawing gore. But after a few tries, he was able to get the hang of it. Pretty soon his stuff was as bad as everyone else's.

Even then, though, even as he was drawing the snarling faces and chewed up victims, a part of him felt kind of uneasy. He wasn't sure how or why . . . but somehow, some way, a part of him knew it was wrong.

It wasn't a big feeling. No shouting voices, no flashing neon signs. Instead, it was kind of a quiet, almost queasy feeling. Some people would call it his conscience. Nick and his folks would say it was God. In any case, if Nick wanted to, he could ignore that feeling. He could let all the excitement and good times drown it out. . . .

And since that's what he wanted, that's what he did. The uneasy feeling disappeared almost as quickly as it had come. He'd pay attention to it some other time. Right now, he was going to go along with the gang. Just now, he'd let them slap him on the back and tell him how good his gore was.

On the way home everyone was still talking about the film—especially Louis. "The soundtrack to the movie is by Death Threat!" he exclaimed.

The kids on the bus all nodded in approval. Renee, not to be outdone, threw in her two-cents' worth. "I've seen all the Freak movies," she bragged.

"Seen them?" Louis chirped. "You starred in them!"

Everyone laughed. They usually did whenever Louis zinged someone. Renee gave him the usual roll of her eyes. Still, she had to admit he was pretty sharp.

Finally, the bus pulled to a stop and the doors hissed open. "So what do you think?" Louis asked Nicholas as they headed for the door. "Can you make it to the 2:15 matinee tomorrow?"

"It'll be great!" Nicholas exclaimed as they stepped into the bright sunlight.

But Louis couldn't let it go. Here was another chance to razz Nick about his folks. So, of course, being the good friend he was, Louis did just that.

"Think your mom and dad will let you out of the house?" By the twinkle in Louis's eyes Nicholas knew he was only kidding.

22

Still, Nick had a reputation to keep up. He didn't want Louis to think he was some wimp who always had to check with his folks for permission. So Nicholas took a chance. Or, rather, he took a guess. . . .

"Hey, I can handle my folks. No sweat."

"All right!" Louis high-fived Nick and they headed for their homes.

When Nick threw open the back door to his house everyone was in a panic. Sarah was running around looking for an empty box. Mom was shouting orders from the hallway. Little sister Jamie sat on the kitchen stool looking very frightened.

"What happened? What's wrong?" Nicholas asked with concern.

Jamie looked at him. She tried to speak, but she could only get out a loud sniff.

"Mom!" Sarah shouted from the basement. "We've got this old apple crate. Will that do?"

"That's fine!" Mom called. "Grab a beach towel and put it in the bottom so he'll be comfortable."

"What's going on?" Nicholas asked louder.

Suddenly Mom came bursting into the room. In her arms was Whatever. But instead of being his usual cheery, obnoxious self, he lay very still and very quiet. Only an occasional whimper escaped him

"It's Whatever," Mom explained. "There's something wrong with his stomach."

"Oh, Mom. . . ." Jamie started to cry.

"It's OK, Pumpkin. The vet will be able to do something. I'm sure of it." Mom tried her best to stay cool and calm. Jamie tried her best to believe her. Even so, the way Mom raced around the kitchen it was obvious she was pretty concerned.

"Honey," she said, turning to Nicholas. "Will you get the door for me?"

"Sure, Mom." He crossed to the door and opened it. "What happened?"

"Sarah!" Mom called.

"Coming!" Sarah's voice was closer as she raced up the stairs.

"I don't know," Mom said in answer to Nick's question. "Maybe he got into some poison. Maybe it's something he ate. I don't know."

Just then Sarah appeared from the stairs with the apple crate and a beach towel. By the look on her face it was pretty obvious she knew what had happened—and by the look she shot Nicholas it was pretty obvious she knew he knew. . . .

The chicken bone.

Jamie was crying louder now. She was trying her best not to. For a seven-year-old she was doing a pretty good job. Still, she was only seven—and seven meant tears.

"Oh, Pumpkin, he'll be OK," Mom said, then she turned to Sarah. "Fold the towel and set it inside."

Sarah obeyed, then Mom gently lifted Whatever and carefully set him in the box.

"There you go, boy," she said.

The dog looked up and gave a pitiful little whimper. He looked awful.

Sarah's eyes were starting to burn. She bit her lip to hold back her tears.

24

"Nicholas," Mom said, "Dad should be home any minute. Watch Jamie for me till he gets here."

"Sure."

She gave him a weak little smile as she passed on her way out the door. "Sarah, are you coming?"

Sarah was right behind her. She didn't say a word. She wouldn't even look at Nick. She just stared at the ground and headed out the door.

Nicholas watched silently as they climbed into the car with Whatever and pulled away.

Sarah's voice was crystal clear in his memory: *Don't sweat it; he loves chicken. One piece isn't going to hurt him.*

After X-raying Whatever, the veterinarian knew the dog had swallowed something. Probably a bone. The doctor wasn't sure whether she'd have to operate or not. Either way, Whatever would have to spend the night.

On the way home in the car, Sarah finally admitted what she had done. "He loves chicken so much," she blurted. "I just couldn't say no."

Mom tried her best to understand, but she was pretty upset. So was Dad when they got home and told him what had happened. How could Sarah be so irresponsible? Didn't she know what the chicken bones would do?

Sarah did know, and she was more than a little sorry. In fact, she was feeling so bad that Mom and Dad decided to go easy on her.

By the time they'd finished dinner, things had cooled down quite a bit. Enough, Nicholas had hoped, that he could ask about seeing the movie. The timing couldn't have been better. Sarah was over at the table doing her homework. Mom was in the kitchen finishing cleaning up. Most important, Dad was upstairs. That was the perfect part! That meant that Mom was separated from him . . . alone . . . vulnerable. When the two of them were together, she was always the softer touch. When she was by herself, well, it would be a piece of cake.

Nick started off by playing it cool and nonchalant, like it was nothing. *With any luck,* he thought, *she'll say yes right off the bat.* But this wasn't Nick's lucky day.

"Absolutely not!" she snapped.

The words fell like a death sentence on his ears. "But, Mom . . ."

"Why would you want to go see a gross movie like that anyway?"

"Cause *he's* gross," Sarah shot back from the table. Now it's true that Sarah was feeling pretty bad about her dog. She was feeling pretty crummy about what she had done. But, hey, she was his older sister. She couldn't let a good put-down like that get by her. After all, she did have a reputation to keep up.

"It's not that bad," Nicholas complained to his mom. But her look made it pretty clear that she'd also seen those TV commercials.

So much for that argument. Nick's brain raced until he found another tactic. It wasn't great, and it wasn't very original—but it was all he had, so he used it: "Besides," he stuttered, "everybody's seeing it."

Immediately he could have kicked himself. How could he be so stupid? He'd left himself wide open for the standard parental comeback. Any second those awful dreaded words would be rolling from mom's lips: "Oh? You mean is everybody jumped off a cliff, you would jump, too?"

He had to act and act fast. He'd jump in before she had a chance to use that deadly phrase. He would jump in with his final—and his best—line of attack. He would use all of his cunning, his wisdom, his brilliance.

He would beg.

"Come on, Mom . . . Pleeease . . ."

He gave her his best wide-eyed, puppy-dog look. It was working. He could see she was starting to soften . . . to break. He had her! Now he'd go in for the kill! Now he'd finish her off with—

"Please what?" a voice asked from the kitchen doorway.

Oh no! It was Dad! Where'd he come from? No fair! Foul! Foul! But it was too late. He had come in to grab a soda from the refrigerator, and his timing couldn't have been worse.

"Nicholas wants to go see a movie with Louis," Mom said.

"Sure, why not?" Dad asked as he poked his head in the fridge.

Nick held his breath. This was it. It could go either way. If Dad just didn't ask the other question—the one that always came up when they talked about movies. If he just didn't ask . . .

"What's it rated?" Aargh! He asked it! That was it. Nick was dead. He knew it.

But instead of an answer, everything was silent. Could it be? Could it be that nobody was going to tell? If no one answered, maybe the question would go away. Chances were good. . . . Dad was busy looking for his diet cream soda. . . . Maybe he wouldn't notice he hadn't gotten an answer. If everybody stayed quiet, then maybe, just maybe, Nick could—

"Oh, it's a real classic," Sarah piped up.

Nicholas glared at her and wondered what the penalty was for murdering your sister. Maybe they'd go easy on him. I mean, who would mind one less big-mouth sister in the world?

She wasn't done, either. In fact, she was grinning. At last her day had meaning: She could go to bed knowing that once again she had ruined Nicholas's entire life. *"Night of the Blood Freaks—Part IV,"* she told their dad, savoring each word.

Slowly Dad straightened up and looked at Nick over the door of the fridge. Nick tried not to let their eyes meet, but it did no good. He looked at his father pitifully, helplessly. "It's in 3-D," he croaked.

"No way. Absolutely not."

"But, Dad . . ." Nick could feel himself starting to get angry.

"Honey," Mom reasoned, "we don't want you filling your mind with that kind of garbage. You know that."

Now they were coming at him from both sides. "But, Mom . . ."

"I told you so." Sarah couldn't resist getting in another good jab.

Frustrated, Nicholas spun around at her and shouted, "Shut up!"

"Nicholas." Dad's voice was anything but pleased.

"Well . . ." Nick was stuttering, looking for the right words. "Why am I always the one who can't do

28

anything?" His voice was getting high and shrill, a good sign he was losing control.

"Nicholas . . . ," Dad warned.

But it was all coming out now, and there was nothing Nick could do to stop it. "Can't do this; can't do that—"

"One more word out of you, young man—"

"It's not fair," Nicholas shouted over his dad. "Everybody else gets to go out—"

"Nichol—" Mom tried to stop him from getting in any worse hot water, but Nick was too busy shouting to hear.

"Everybody else gets to go, but I have to sit around with a bunch of old—"

"That's it!" Dad's voice was sharp and to the point. It immediately brought Nicholas to a stop. He'd gone too far, and he knew it.

Dad continued firm and even. "We don't talk that way in this home. Now go to your room. You're grounded."

Nicholas couldn't believe his ears. Grounded! How could this have gone so wrong?

He looked at Dad. The man stood solid and firm. Then he looked at his mom. She was also holding her ground.

Nick felt his ears start to burn, his head start to pound. He was so mad he felt like exploding, but what could he do? His dad had spoken. And by the tone in his voice and the look in his eyes, Nick knew he meant every word of it.

Nicholas Martin, Mr. I-can-handle-my-folks-no-sweat, was grounded—and there was nothing he could do about it.

Finally he snapped around and started for the stairs. It was so unfair. *All* of it!

He reached the bottom of the steps and started to

stomp up them—loudly. He might not be able to say anything more, but no one had said anything about stomping.

Mom and Dad looked on. Neither was happy about having to ground Nicholas. Unfortunately, he'd given them no choice.

FOUR
Everybody's a Critic

Parents. Yeah, you know who they are. The folks that hang
around your house telling you when to walk, talk, and
jump—and how high. The big guys who always hand out
orders like "Take out the trashEat your vegetablesTake a
bathPractice your tubaStop practicing your tubaDon't pick at
itChange your socksClean up your roomGet a haircut" . . . and
about a thousand other things that you hate to do.

But, hey, they can't help it. That's their job. Everyone knows
parents are supposed to make you do all those things and
prevent you from having fun.

Oh, yeah. They're best at that—at preventing you from
having fun. Like when you want to go skateboarding down the
freeway with Tom, Dick, and Harry. The answer is always no:
"No, you'll get run over. Skateboard around the house, where
it's safe."

OK, so it's a pain to stay home while Tom, Dick, and Harry
get to skateboard down the freeway. But hey, like I always say,
it's easier to stay home than wind up a pancake under some
semi's rear tire.

Besides, I've noticed something interesting. Nick's folks
usually only put the clamps on him when his "fun" is gonna
end up creaming him. I know, it doesn't make being clamped

31

any easier. But I've got a pretty good hunch that's how it is with most parents.

Shucks, parents are bound to know something. I don't think you can get that job unless you've been around and learned some things. Unfortunately, convincing my buddy Nick of that wasn't easy.

Dad and Mom had just dropped the big one on Nick's plans for Night of the Blood Freaks. He had lost the war—big time. Not only was he forbidden to see the gross-out flick with Louis, but his "diplomacy" had landed him in the clink. He came stomping into the bedroom, mad at the world, just as I was getting ready for bed and brushing my teeth.

I decided to take pity on my pal, maybe enlighten him in the workings of parent-child relationships. Of course, this meant I was going to have to think like an adult. Not an easy task, but I figured I'd give it a shot.

As Nick wrestled with his shirt and kicked off his shoes, I began my approach. "Hey, Nick," I started off cheerfully.

"Ah, go smell your socks," he barked.

"Wound a bit tightly tonight, aren't we?" I kidded.

But he just kept yanking his clothes off as if they were on fire and pounced down on the bed in a boiling heap of frustration.

"Look, kid," I said, trying to reason with him. "You watch movies like that long enough, and pretty soon they'll stick a sign on your head that says Dump Site."

"What are you, some kind of film critic?" he scoffed as he tucked back the covers and crawled into bed.

"Well, as a matter of fact . . ."

Suddenly we were sitting in a deserted theater balcony (ain't imagination grand?). I was crammed into a snug-fitting V-neck

32

sweater and an equally tight pair of polyester slacks. Nick was in an open-collar dress shirt and a well-fitting navy blazer. We had become the Dynamic Duo of movie criticdom: Roger Beefer and Gene Dismal, the cohosts of TV's Let's Mangle the Movies.

"Well, Gene," I said, "let's take a look at our next clip, The Molting Falcon. OK, roll it." Nothing happened. "Roll it! Roll it already!"

Finally the screen began to flicker, and the movie began. . . .

"My name is Shade," the leading man said (an outstanding award-winning actor who bears an uncanny resemblance to yours truly). "Spam Shade, Private Eye. I was relaxing in my second-story office on the lower East Side: the lower, lower East Side. It was so low the snails wore elevator shoes just to stay on the sidewalks. Even so, it's wasn't as low as I was feeling.

"I was down. I had been working two weeks, night and day, on a case that was really a tough nut to crack. (Actually, it was a walnut. I'd used a hammer, a pair of pliers, and a screw-driver, and I still hadn't gotten the thing open. A guy could starve to death. Next Christmas I hoped Aunt Nellie would send me a fruitcake instead.) I sat back in my chair and took a stout swig of my diet soda.

"Then she walked in.

"She stepped into the place like she owned the joint. She leaned against the doorway and drew out a cigarette. I guess she didn't notice the No Smoking sign. Being a gentleman, I was gonna offer her a light. Then I saw she had one. A blow torch.

"She lit up the room. As a matter of fact, she lit up the coatrack. We put the fire out; then I asked her her name. 'Thelma,' she said. She was the kind of babe your mom warned you about. That's OK, though. Mom was in Cleveland getting a nose job. So I asked Thelma to take a seat.

33

"She sat down, then said she was looking for her bird, a molting falcon. She whipped out a half-charred photo and handed it to me. It was a picture of her and the bird standing in front of Old Geezer, the world famous waterspout in Yellow Phones National Park. The bird was wearing a polka-dot tie. It looked like they had been on vacation. . . . I was beginning to think they were also out to lunch.

"Thelma said the bird had disappeared around the docks. She thought the whole thing smelled kind of fishy. I wondered what she expected the docks to smell like.

"Well, it just so happened I had been down at the docks earlier and found just such a bird. I whipped it out of my drawer. The tie matched, and so did the bird. Too bad it was dead now.

"Just then I heard a blood-curdling scream accompanied by a loud thud. It was Thelma, passed out on the floor. I guess she was the sensitive type. Either that or it was time for her afternoon nap.

"Oh well, that wraps up another thrilling case for Spam Shade, Private Eye."

The lights in the theater came up, and I turned to my partner. "You know, Gene," I said, "they just don't make films like that anymore. Great story, great dialogue—and a particularly great performance by the lead. I give this flick a thumbs up."

"No way," Roger said. "If that film was any flatter, it would be in the House of Pancakes. Now if you want to see a really great flick, let's take a look at the new remake, starring that action-packed performer, Flint Streethood. OK, roll it."

Now, folks, as near as I can tell, this film had something to do with somebody being mad at somebody about something, *and it's just as well you never see it. Still, let me see if I can describe what happened.*

Some guy carrying a gun the size of a B-52 bomber walked into a drugstore and said, "OK, punk, make my parfait." The next thing I know, everybody was shooting at everybody else. It went something like this:

Kapow! Kapow! Blam! Blam! Whir! Bang! Bang! Bang! Rat-tat-tat-tat-tat-tat-tat-tat! Kaboom! Kawham! Bang! Cough! Cough! Kak-kak-kak-kak! Wheeze! Wheeze! Kagang! Kagang! Whir! Whir! Pop!

Are you getting the idea? The last thing I remember was a grenade coming straight out of the screen and—KaWHOOM!

"You call that fun?!" I gasped. The blast had blown us clear out of our make-believe theater and back to the bedroom— which was fine with me. "Why don't you just stick your head in a garbage can?"

"Because then I would have to room with you," Nick said with a cough as he reached for the light next to the bedpost. "Let's just try to get some sleep."

Well, at least he's forgotten about the silly *Blood Freak* flick, *I thought*. Then again, who knows? Tomorrow is another day, and boys will be boys. *Or will they?*

FIVE
Cyborg's Plan

By 9:00 the next morning, things had started to look
a little better. Not perfect, mind you, but a little better.
For starters, it was Saturday. And Saturday meant, you
guessed it, no school!

It's not that Nicholas hated school. It's just that he
could think of a lot better ways to spend six hours a day,
which according to his calculations meant:

6 hours x 5 days = 30 hours a week!
30 hours x 4 weeks = 120 hours a month!
120 hours x 9 months = 1,080 hours a year!

1,080 hours a year in school! Awful! Terrible! Of course,
Nick ignored the fact that the only reason he could do
those calculations was because he had spent so much
time in school.

Anyway, another reason Saturday morning looked
better was that Nick had cooled down some. As usual, his
talk with McGee had helped. Not that he agreed with the
little munchkin. Hardly. But he was able to understand
a little more where his folks were coming from. Only
a little, though.

Another good thing was the news on Whatever. The vet called bright and early that morning to say that everything was fine. There was no need to operate. In fact, they could pick him up anytime they wanted.

Of course, Sarah had her dad talked into going down there in no time flat. She was feeling pretty good. In fact, she was feeling so good that she started to make excuses about giving Whatever the bone. They were barely out of the garage before she had herself convinced that it wasn't even her fault.

"I was just doing the loving thing," she insisted. "You couldn't expect me to be some old ogre and say no, could you? I mean, not when I love him?"

Dad could only shake his head at her logic. "It's because you love him that I'd expect you to say no," he explained.

Sarah looked at him, confused.

"Sweetheart," he continued, "just because you love someone doesn't always mean you let him have his way. I mean, look at Nicholas."

"I'd rather not," she cracked.

Dad ignored the comment. "Nick wanted to see that movie—but we knew it was bad for him."

"You mean with all the blood and gore and junk?"

"Right. Seeing that movie would be as bad for Nick's mind as that chicken bone was for Whatever's stomach."

"OK . . . so . . ."

"So," Dad continued, "which would have shown him more love? Letting him go off and do something that would hurt him, or saying no and letting him be angry at us?"

"I guess saying no."

Dad nodded.

Sarah was starting to see the picture . . . and for once she didn't have a comeback. Well, she always had a comeback. This one just wasn't great. "It's hard to say no," she insisted. "I mean, you know how Whatever loves chicken."

"It's hard for us to say no to you guys, too. If we had it our way, we'd always say yes. We'd always give you what you wanted. But we see the bigger picture, and because we love you . . . well, sometimes we have to be the heavy and say no."

Sarah looked out the window. After a long moment, she said, "Being a parent doesn't always sound so easy."

"No kidding!" Dad exclaimed.

Sarah turned back to him and grinned. "It has its rewards, though, doesn't it?"

A puzzled look came across her dad's face. "Well," he said, "if you hear of any, let me know."

"Daddy!" Sarah gave him a poke in the ribs, and he broke into a grin.

It's too bad Nicholas hadn't heard that conversation. Maybe his decision would have been different when Louis called. . . .

"Hello?"

"Hey, Nick." Louis's voice was a little thick and raspy from the morning, but Nicholas immediately recognized it. "You ready for the flick?"

Oh no, Nick thought. He'd forgotten all about his promise to Louis. Not only would he have to explain why he couldn't go, but now he'd have to go through all of Louis's jabs and jokes about how strict his parents were. To make it worse, his mother was standing three feet away at the kitchen sink. Well, better to get it over with, quick and simple. . . .

"I can't go."

"What?" Louis asked.

"I'm grounded."

"Grounded?" Louis knew Nick's parents were strict—but not that strict. "How are you going to the show if you're grounded?"

"I can't."

"Oh, man . . . ," Louis sighed.

It wasn't easy for Mom to hear this conversation. She knew how important the movie was to Nick. She could tell how embarrassed he was. Still . . . she also knew how rude he'd been the night before. Even more important, she knew how harmful the movie would be.

Unfortunately, the wheels inside Louis's brain were turning. An idea was coming to his beady little brain. "Hold it. Wait a minute," he said. "Wait a minute . . . 'Blue Fox Leader?'"

"Huh?" Nick didn't get it. What did the TV series have to do with his being grounded? How was that going to help him see the movie?

"Remember last week's episode?" Louis asked. "Remember the plan Cyborg II used to free Blue Fox Leader from the dreaded Black Tower?"

It took Nicholas a moment to catch on. Then he remembered the show . . . he remembered how Cyborg and Blue Fox used their telecommunicators, how Cyborg distracted the Scorpion-tailed android guards so Blue Fox could make his escape. Most important, he remembered how Blue Fox used his superior creativity to build a decoy.

"Superior creativity. Hmmmmm." That was right up Nicholas's alley. He cast a guarded look at his mom and slid out of earshot as he and Louis worked out their plan. . . .

First Nick attached the toilet plunger.

It took some doing, but with Crazy Glue and the right amount of suction, Nick was able to make it stick onto the inside of his bedroom door.

Next came the electrical cable. Sure, it looked like a lot of twisted-up Christmas tree lights. And he probably didn't need them all blinking. But, hey, that was part of the effect. He hooked one end of the cable to a small sensor on the plunger. Then he attached the other end to a cassette player on his bed.

Now for the recorded message. Nick was careful to make his voice sound just bored enough.

For the normal kid, this stuff would be pretty hard to do. Nicholas, however, was no normal kid. He has this imagination that just wouldn't stop. You could see it in all of his McGee drawings. You could see it in his automatic walnut cracker. You could see it in his light-activated door opener. Today, though, he'd outdone himself. Today he'd created the Fool-your-parents-so-they-think-you're-still-in-your-room invention.

The last step was the lightbulb. He screwed it into the socket attached to the plunger. Then Nick hesitated for a moment. This was it. Would it really work? He took a deep breath and gently knocked on the door.

The bulb lit! It was a success! *All right!*

It had taken him nearly two hours. Two hours of rummaging for parts in the garage, the basement, the attic . . . and then there were all those delicate electrical hook-ups. Finally, though, he was finished. And it actually worked!

Just in time, too. Almost immediately his walkie-talkie began to beep. It had to be Louis.

Nicholas picked it up and said, "Cyborg II, this is Blue Fox Leader. Do you copy?"

For a moment there was no answer, and Nick's heart began to sink. Without Louis the plan would not work. Without Louis he couldn't possibly sneak out. Without Louis—

"Roger, Blue Fox. I'm reading you loud and clear."

Nick broke into a grin.

Louis was outside, hiding in the front yard. He was trying his best to look like the super-intelligent and ever-so-wise Cyborg II. Unfortunately, he didn't quite make it.

Maybe it was his clothes. Maybe it was the pulled-down stocking cap, the thick scarf, and the heavy sweatshirt. Or maybe it was all the sweat he was covered with from wearing those cloths in the eighty-degree weather. In any case, Louis looked more like a crazed bag lady than the all-knowing hero from Kalugrium.

That didn't stop him, though. Not one bit. Fantasy was fantasy, and he planned to play this one to the hilt.

"Synchronize watches to 11:28," Louis continued, "and lets commence execution."

"Execution?" The word caught Nicholas off guard. Until now it had all been fun and games; it really hadn't been real . . . but "execution" sounded an awful lot like punishment. And punishment would definitely be part of Nick's future if he were caught. After all, he was disobeying his parents—and in a *big* way.

Reality only lasted a second, though. Louis soon brought Nick back to his senses.

"Yeah. Execute the plan. You know, 'the plan.'"

"Oh, uh, right . . . the plan."

Nicolas grinned as he pushed down the antenna and threw on his coat. Everything was going great! Everything had been worked out. There would be no problems.

Or so he thought . . .

Tsk, tsk, tsk . . . "What a tangled web we weave when we prac-i-tac-tice to deceive." That's what I always say. And that's exactly what my good buddy Nick was doing. He thought he was being quite the clever escape artist with all those electronic gizmos and wires running every which way.

I must admit his creativity in the matter was quite impressive. His electronic doodads gave a realistic impression that he was calmly sketching in his room. Well, everybody else might be fooled, but not me.

I don't know. It seemed like a lot of wasted effort to fool his parents just so he could go and be grossed out. Why didn't he just go downstairs and make a broccoli and stewed prune sandwich? Always works for me.

Besides, seems to me Nick should devote his time to more rewarding activities. You know, challenging endeavors that would spark his mind and spirit. Things that would help him

be a better person. Things like . . . well, you know . . . like
clipping his toenails.

Yeah. That's it. If he would clip his toenails on a regular
basis, it would . . . well, it would . . . OK, it wouldn't do
anything. But since it was what I was doing at the time,
I thought it was pretty worthwhile.

Still, as preoccupied with that task as I was (after all,
I didn't want to cut off my big toe or something), I decided it
was time to tell Nick how I felt about his little rendezvous with
Louis. "You'll be sorry," I said, continuing to trim away at my
tootsies.

"Aren't you coming?" Nick asked.

Obviously, he knew if I played along with his clever little
scheme, he'd have a better chance of pulling it off. But I didn't
want any part of it. "Uh-uh, no way," I said in a superior
tone. "I got principles, I got convictions." I leaped to my feet
and began to sing, "I got rhythm. . . . "

But Nick wasn't the least bit impressed. He just stood there
for a second, until a sly grin crossed his face. He had an idea,
I could tell. But it wouldn't work. No matter what he said,
I was going to make him realize how I felt about this whole
underhanded plot. Nothing was going to change my mind. So I
just kept on singing, "I got rhythm. . . . "

"I'll give you a dollar," he offered.

"I got . . . to get my shoes," I said.

OK, so I gave in. Can I help it I was flat busted and would
do anything for a buck? Well, at least I'll have a little walking money for the show, *I thought. Although all you can get*
at the movies for a buck these days is a cup of ice and half a
Milk Dud.

Nick made some final adjustments on his Fool-your-folks

*invention while I laced up my glow-in-the-dark tennis shoes.
(I like to see where I'm walking in those dark theaters.)*

*We both stood there a second, took a deep breath, then
cautiously crept out of the bedroom door.*

*I sure hoped this stupid plan worked. Or we would end up
in worse shape than any of the victims in this freak flick ever
thought about.*

SIX
The Escape!

Carefully Blue Fox ("Nick" to his friends) moved down
the stairs. Who knew where his enemies lurked? Who
knew what dastardly tortures he would face if caught?
It didn't matter, though, for his courage was great. Yes,
the courage of Blue Fox Leader was beyond compare.

Unfortunately, there was only one way out—through
the Control Center of the enemy's fortress (which, to
untrained eyes, looks a lot like a kitchen).

Thanks to months of training, Blue Fox knew exactly
which steps creaked and which didn't. With expert
wisdom he avoided those hidden alarms, which had
obviously been placed by the enemy to alert them in case
he tried to escape.

As he approached the Control Center, he could hear
the murmur of an alien voice. With each step the voice
grew louder. By it's higher pitch, Blue Fox could tell it was
the Female Unit, the second in command. Fortunately,
the Supreme Commander was out back spray-painting
some patio furniture.

Carefully Blue Fox peeked around the corner of the
stairs. There she was . . . the Female. She was talking on
the phone to the counseling center. Across the counter in

the family room, Blue Fox could see the Female Unit's mother. They called her Grandma for short. She had her back to him and was knitting. Probably some phaser-proof vest for one of the Offspring.

Ah, yes. The Offspring!

Quickly Blue Fox scanned the area. Fortunately the Offspring were nowhere to be found. Good. Well, good and bad. Good because it meant Blue Fox would not have to sneak past them. (The Offsprings' senses were much keener than those of the Older Units.) Bad because the Offspring were just the kind of creatures who would suddenly swoop in from nowhere and catch him out in the open.

This was not a time for fear, though. This was a time for action. Blue Fox knew he had to cross the Control Center. That meant the Female Unit must be removed. Blue Fox pulled back out of sight. Quickly he keyed in his tele-communicator.

"Cyborg II, Cyborg II, this is Blue Fox Leader," he whispered. "Emergency at kitchen, Request diversionary tactics."

Louis was still outside hiding in the front yard when his buddy's called for help came. All right! This was what he'd been waiting for! He answered, "Roger, Blue Fox. I'm on my way."

Like a shot, he jumped up from behind the concrete wall and headed for the front porch. It was a dangerous mission. Any moment he could be spotted by the enemy and demolecularized (you know, melted into a little puddle of loose atoms). That didn't matter, though, because that was his friend in there. That was the great

Blue Fox Leader. And if there was one thing Cyborg II was famous for, it was his loyalty.

Inside, Blue Fox pressed himself flat against the stairway wall and waited. Would Cyborg II complete his mission?

It had been tricky, and Cyborg II had had more than one close call. Finally, though, he reached the stairs of the front porch. Just in time, too, for a motorized vehicle (that earthlings would call a "car") came crashing around the corner. Cyborg II dropped behind the bushes out of sight as it passed.

Then, summoning all his strength and courage, Cyborg II rose from hiding, glanced about, and raced up the stairs toward the front door, where he reached out and rang the doorbell . . . once, twice. Then he darted down the steps as quickly as he had come.

When he heard the doorbell, Blue Fox grinned, Cyborg II had not let him down. Furthermore, the plan had the desired effect upon the Female Unit.

"Uh, Mary Ann?"the Female Unit said into the phone. "Can you hold on? There's somebody at the door."

Blue Fox heard her set the phone down on the counter and push open the hallway door. Perfect!

Now it was time to make his move!

He started across the kitchen, planning to go through the family room and out the other door. With any luck he'd go completely undetected.

So much for luck . . .

"Sarah . . . ," he heard the Female Unit call from the

hallway. "Can you see who that is at the door?" Then the hallway door started to open.

Oh no! What should he do!? The Female Unit was coming back in, and he was trapped out in the open! Then he spotted it—the control console, cleverly disguised as one of those stove tops built in the middle of the kitchen. It wasn't very big, but it would have to do. He dove for cover just as the door opened.

Blue Fox held his breath, waiting. He was crouched on one side of the little kitchen island, and the Female Unit was standing on the other. They were less than four feet apart.

She picked up the phone and started talking again. For a moment, Blue Fox was safe. Well, not quite. True to form, the Female Unit liked to keep busy. There was a long cord on the phone, so she could move all around the kitchen as she talked.

Suddenly Blue Fox heard her approaching footsteps. Oh no! She was heading right for him! Quickly he scrambled on his hands and knees to the opposite side.

He made it just as she rounded the corner. It was close, but he was safe.

Suddenly the Female Unit changed directions and headed the opposite way. Blue Fox frantically switched into reverse and backed up. Then she changed directions again, and so did he. It looked like some strange sort of dance as she unknowingly chased him around the little island . . . first one direction, than the other, and then the first direction again.

Blue Fox Leader was beginning to feel a little ridiculous . . . not to mention a lot dizzy.

Finally the Female Unit finished her conversation and hung up the phone. Then Blue Fox Leader heard it . . . that wonderful sound of the squeaky kitchen door being opened again.

"Sarah?" the Female Unit called. "Sarah, who was at the door?"

Perfect! She was out of the room. Blue Fox rose to his feet and started for the family room door, only to dive again for cover as the Offspring threw it open. "Mother?"

Now Blue Fox Leader was at the end of the kitchen counter—the one that separated the kitchen from the family room. And if that wasn't bad enough, Female Unit suddenly came back through the kitchen door. "Oh, there you are."

What is this, a convention? Blue Fox thought. It was crazy. The Female Unit was on one side of the counter, and the Offspring was on the other. While he, the great Blue Fox Leader, was trapped in between. All either of them had to do was cross three feet down his way, and bingo, they'd spot him.

"Who was at the door?" the Female Unit asked.

"No one," the Offspring answered.

"Probably one of those silly kids."

"But, Mom," the Offspring cracked. "Nicholas is upstairs."

For a moment Nick thought it was unfair that the real Blue Fox Leader didn't have to put up with a sister.

"Grandma?" The Offspring turned toward the sofa with the Older Unit. "Can you help me with the curtains in my room?"

"Well, sure, dear," the Older Unit answered.

Blue Fox heard the creak of the sofa as she rose to her feet. "How do they look?" she asked. "Is the length OK?"

Great! They were heading toward the door.

"Well, kind of," the Offspring answered. "But it's uneven at the bottom."

"We'll take care of that," the Older Unit said as the door creaked open and their voices faded down the hall.

Super! Now it was just Blue Fox and the Female Unit!

He leaned back and looked over his shoulder. She was at the counter starting to make some peanut-butter-and-jelly nutrition packets. Silently he dropped to his knees and inched his way around to the family room side of the counter.

The doorway lay just ahead. All he had to do was quietly crawl toward the door. . . .

Carefully he crept forward. Foot by foot, inch by inch. All the time he could hear the Female Unit just above his head, on the other side, preparing the meal. Closer and closer the door came. He was nearly there.

A good thing, too. The game was starting to wear on Nicholas. It had started off fun enough, but all this sneaking, this hiding, this disobeying . . . well, it was definitely starting to take its toll on him. A tight knot of guilt had started growing in his stomach, and it was growing bigger by the second.

Finally he reached his hand out to the door. Soon it would be over. Then the worst happened. He was spotted—by a four-legged hairball. It was the Offspring's pesky pooch! And worse yet, the carnivorous canine thought Blue Fox wanted to play. So he began to bark.

Blue Fox tried to shush him. He tried to silence him.

The animal just took it as a sign of encouragement. He'd just spent the last twelve hours at the vet's, teetering between life and Poochie Paradise. Now that he was OK, he figured it was time to party.

"What on earth?"the Female Unit leaned over the counter toward the dog. She was directly above Blue Fox's head but could not see him. "Whatever—are you all right, boy?"

The dog continued to bark.

"Whatever . . . what's wrong, fella?" Her voice sounded more concerned.

Oh no! Any minute she'd set down her knife and cross into the family room to check out the problem. Maybe she thought he was still sick. Maybe she thought he was having a relapse. Either way, once she crossed around the counter, she would spot the great Blue Fox Leader!

Desperately, Blue Fox looked for a solution. Anything—he'd even settle for a chicken bone right now. There was nothing.

Well . . . almost nothing . . .

Have you ever noticed this? That in the most critical moment of a daring and dangerous escape plan, when the safety of the entire free world rides on split-second timing, there's always some mangy mutt hanging around who starts barking his head off? Which, of course, alerts everyone from Cleveland to Crabwell Corners of your presence. Have you ever noticed that?

It happens every time. In fact, it was happening right now to my good buddy, Nick.

53

Whatever, the family fur ball, was only seconds away from blowing our movie mission. The half-witted hound's persistent barking had to go; otherwise Nicholas would probably replace this pooch in the doghouse.

What old Rover needed was a little game of fetch, commando style. I whipped out a nice, round, black bomb, which I keep for such occasions, and lit the fuse. Nick gave me a look of alarm. I think he was afraid I was about to give this pup a permanent toothache. Of course, that wasn't the plan.

I gave Nick a reassuring wink, then beckoned to Whatever with the burning bomb. "Come here, boy," I called, slapping my thigh and giving a soft whistle, waving the bomb around like a fine turkey bone.

The dorky dog stopped barking and stepped forward hesitantly. Hooray for curiosity.

I continued to sweet-talk the critter, until he finally sniffed at the fizzling fuse. Just as I had hoped, a spark flew out and smacked Whatever right on the nose. The chickenhearted cat-chaser turned tail and raced through the kitchen and up the stairs, yelping all the way.

Mom, somewhat startled, dropped what she was doing and followed in hot pursuit. "Whatever, are you OK? Come here. Come here, fellow. Whatever?"

Nick heaved a sigh of relief. "Thanks," he whispered.

I licked my fingers and pinched out the burning fuse. "It will cost you another seventy-five cents," I said calmly.

Nick looked annoyed. But, hey, that had been a pretty desperate situation. Besides, the extra cash would come in handy at the show. Now I could get a whole Milk Dud.

Nick rose to his feet, shot a glance around the room, then

crept out of the kitchen. "Let's go," he whispered to me over his shoulder.

This movie had better be worth it, *I thought as I followed him out of the kitchen.* Or I'm going to charge him another quarter when we get home.

By the time Nick made it outside. He was exhausted. All that sneaking around had worn him out. Besides, that little knot of guilt in his stomach was now about the size of a baseball. Needless to say, he was glad the game was finally over.

Well, almost.

Louis was still wearing his stocking cap. His scarf was still pulled up over his face, and he was still using their walkie-talkie. Nick may have been done with the game, but Louis had only begun.

"C'mon," Louis whispered. "Follow me."

Nicholas glanced around. "Why are we whispering?"

"Shhhh."

Louis turned—and fell over the garbage cans beside them. They clanked and rattled and banged, making all sorts of racket. Some of the neighborhood dogs started barking.

The two boys pressed flat against the wall just as Mom stuck her head out the front door to have a look. She saw nothing.

"Strange," she said as she finally turned to shut the door, "Very strange."

The boys relaxed, but Nick's heart was beating like a jackhammer. Louis glanced around, then turned to Nicholas and whispered, "Meet me over by that Buick."

"Louis," Nicholas sighed. "Let's just go to the theater." He was sick of the game . . . and he was sick of all the guilt he was feeling.

"What are you talking about?" Louis demanded. "That's not what Blue Fox would do."

"No, and Blue Fox's mom wouldn't chase him around the kitchen either."

Let's just stick to the plan," Louis urged. With that he dashed off.

Nicholas swallowed hard. He wanted to be a good sport, but he also wanted to get rid of the guilt he was feeling. I mean, here his folks were trusting him, expecting him to obey . . . and look what he was doing. It felt terrible. That baseball lying in his stomach was now the size of a volleyball. He took a deep breath, muttered something about not remembering a Buick in the plan, and finally took off.

SEVEN
Attack of the Blood Freaks

The boys had plenty of time to walk to the theater. But superheroes never walk. They dash, dart, or zip. So Louis made sure they did just that . . . all the way.

By the time they finally reached the theater, Nicholas wasn't sure if the pain in his gut was from the guilt or from all the running. Either way, it felt bad. And it was getting worse.

Finally, there it was. The theater. And up on the marquee, in glorious dripping red, was the title: *Night of the Blood Freaks, Part IV*.

Nicholas swallowed hard. He had come this far. There was no backing out now. Then a thought struck him.

"Wait a minute, Louis," he said. "How are we supposed to get in if we're not old enough?"

Not to worry. The great Cyborg II had already figured out a plan. "No problem," he said with a grin. "Follow me." With that, he took off for the ticket line.

Nicholas swallowed again. By this time, though, there wasn't much left to swallow. His mouth was as dry as the Sahara desert. Numbly, he turned and followed his friend to the back of the line.

Interestingly enough, the back of the line doesn't stay

the back to the line forever. Nick saw that they were moving closer and closer toward the box office window. Any second they'd be there. Any second Nick's crime would be found out. Any second SWAT teams would appear, arrest him, and throw him in jail for life. Or, worse yet, he'd be forced to listen to one of his dad's lectures.

Closer and closer they came. Why had he agreed to this? What had he been thinking of?

Now the man in front of them stepped up to the window. He was average looking—Greek or maybe Arab. Not a bad sort of fellow. He paid for his ticket and moved off.

It was their turn.

Nicholas looked up to the box office attendant. She was kind of pretty, but he didn't notice. He was paralyzed. He couldn't move. He couldn't speak.

Fortunately, Louis could. And he did. Beautifully. "Two, please," he said. Then, turning to the man who had just left, he called out, "Wait up . . . Dad."

A stroke of genius! A brilliant plan! In one sentence Louis had solved all of their problems. Those three little words would get them in, free and clear. Fantastic! Except for one minor problem—"Dad" was Greek; Louis was black.

The box office attendant frowned down at them. Always thinking, Louis pointed to Nicholas. "His dad," he said, reaching in to grab the tickets and head after the man.

"Whew, that was close," Louis whispered to Nicholas . . . but Nicholas was not there. He was still frozen in front of the box office, a pathetic little smile pasted on his face.

Louis took a step back, grabbed him by the collar, and yanked him toward the door.

Back at home, Mom was feeling pretty proud of her son. Nick had taken his punishment so well. He really was a wonderful kid. Not one word of complaint from him all morning. In fact, she hadn't heard any word from him for several hours. She decided to swing up to his room and say hi, and tell him how proud she was of him. Then maybe, just maybe, the whole family could get out later and do something together. Maybe pizza. Maybe miniature golf. Maybe both.

She knocked gently on his door and waited.

Her "wonderful" son's little invention—the one he had spent so much time hooking up—finally went into operation.

Mom's knock started it all by lighting up the light on the door. This sent electricity down the long cable of Christmas tree lights to the cassette recorder. The power snapped the recorder on play, and suddenly Mom heard Nick's voice-recorder but loud and clear: "Who is it?"

"It's Mom," she said from the other side.

"I'm drawing right now," Nick's voice said. "Could you come back later?"

"All right, hon," Mom said, and she left his door with a smile.

What a terrific kid. Other children might have sulked or stayed mad. Not Nicholas. He took his medicine like a real trooper. What a kid. What a delight.

Mom moved down the hall beaming with pride.

Well, Nicholas was taking his medicine all right. Just not exactly the way Mom thought.

At first things in the theater were OK. Nick had never worn 3-D glasses before, and it was pretty exciting the way the credits seemed to jump off the screen at him. For a few moments the ache in his gut was almost gone, and he was actually glad he'd come.

Then the movie started.

The slimy, half-rotted mutants weren't so bad to look at. In fact, it was kind of fun to watch the way they hobbled across the lawn. And their slurping, sucking noises were more disgusting than scary. It was when they got into the house . . . and what they did to their first victim . . . well, at first it was kind of interesting. Then it got gross. Then more gross. Then, when you were sure it couldn't get any more gross . . . it did.

Nick glanced at Louis. It was hard to see his friend's expression behind those 3-D glasses. Still, Louis was definitely feeling something. I mean, the kid was munching down popcorn faster than Nick had ever seen him eat in his life.

Now the Freaks were starting up the stairs of the house—heading up to find the rest of the family.

It had been nearly half an hour since Mom checked in on Nicholas. She had just gone upstairs to put away laundry, so she figured she'd stop by and give another knock.

"Who is it?" the recorded voice asked. Only this time it started to drag, which made Nick's voice sound very low and slow. Apparently, Nick had forgotten one small element in his perfect plan: He hadn't checked the batteries in the cassette player.

60

Mom frowned. "Honey, it's Mom. Are you OK? You sound—" she searched for the right word—"tired."

No answer.

"Nicholas?"

She knocked again.

Still no answer.

"Nicholas?" Her concern started to grow. She knocked harder, which shook the cable attached to the recorder, which made the delicate little connectors shake loose and short out—which tripped the cassette player into the "record" mode.

"Nicholas, it's Mom. What's going on in there?" More knocking. More shaking. The recorder clicked back into the "play" mode.

Finally, Mom heard an answer from the other side of the door—but not the one she was expecting. "It's Mom," the voice said. "what's going on in there?"

Mom stopped a moment. That sounded like *her* voice. Not only did it sound like her voice—it *was* her voice.

Sarah stuck her head out of her room to see what the fuss was about. "Hey, Mom, what're you doing?"

"What does it look like I'm doing?" she asked. "I'm talking to myself!"

They looked at each other. Something was wrong. Something was definitely wrong.

Then, from the other side of Nick's door, they heard Mom's voice again: "What does it look like I'm doing? I'm talking to myself!"

That did it. Mom turned the knob and threw open the door. "Nicholas, what on earth . . . ?"

There was no Nicholas. There was only her recorded

61

voice, saying, "Nicholas, what on earth" at about three different speeds.

Then she saw it. The light attached to the door. The cable attached to the light. The cassette player attached to the cable. Yes, indeed, another one of Nicholas's marvelous inventions.

At first Mom didn't understand. Then it began to make sense. It was all a trick. A sneaky trick to make them think he was in his room.

But why? Why would Nicholas want to deceive them like this?

She looked around the room and spotted the answer. On the bed. It was the newspaper advertisement for *Night of the Blood Freaks, Part IV*.

Mom was not smiling.

Back at the theater, the Blood Freaks had found that family and began attacking them . . . one at a time. The sounds were awful . . . lots of screaming and choking and gagging. But the sounds were nothing compared to what you watched. What Nicholas watched. What he couldn't take his eyes from.

As he watched, that volleyball came back into his stomach. Only now it wasn't content just to stay in his stomach. It was trying to jump up his throat and out his mouth. Nicholas tried his best to swallow it . . . but the worse the movie got, the harder it was to keep it down.

Finally everybody was killed off. Well, almost everybody. There was still one little member left. The tiny little sister. She cried; she whimpered; she begged . . . but nothing stopped the Blood Freaks. They did to her what they had done to the others. Only worse. Much worse. Much, much worse. Worse than much worse.

Then, just when Nick thought they had finished—just when he reached for his soda and tried to take a sip from his straw to settle his stomach—the Freaks finished their attack with this sickening slurp that sound just like a soda straw getting the last little bit of drink in a cup.

Nick looked at his straw. Suddenly he wasn't so thirsty anymore.

EIGHT
Busted

At last the nightmare was over. The credits ended, and the final words on the screen were:

"Coming soon to a blood bank near you . . . *Blood Feast of the Blood Freaks, Part V.*"

The kids in the audience broke into cheers. Nick couldn't believe it. He glanced around. Everybody looked as sick and pale as he felt. They were wiped out, too—but they were still cheering and clapping. It was like they could hardly wait to get grossed out all over again.

"Great flick, huh?" Louis beamed.

Nick tried to smile, but he wasn't too successful. Louis saw it, and for a second his grin also faded. For a second Nick could see what his friend was really thinking. Louis wasn't feeling so fit either. It lasted only a second, though.

"Hey, Louis," one of the kids from behind poked him in the back. "Wasn't that great the way they got that last kid?"

"Yeah." Louis was grinning again. "Or the way they . . ."

Nick didn't hear the rest of the conversation. Louis joined his friends and headed up the aisle. Everyone was laughing and talking and shouting. Nick just shook his head. No one would admit how frightened or scared they were. It was almost like they were trying too hard to prove they had had a good time.

But Nicholas couldn't fake it. He felt terrible. What had he done? And more important, why had he done it? His folks were right. The show was awful. It was worse than awful. It was garbage. First-rate, triple-A garbage—with a lot of blood thrown in to wash it down.

The walk home took forever. Unfortunately forever wasn't quite long enough. . . .

When Nick rounded the corner of his block, he quickly checked his front yard. No one was there. So far, so good.

He reached the front porch and quietly crept up the steps. At the front door, he gave a careful listen. Nothing. The coast was clear. Maybe he could make it back up to his room without being noticed.

He opened the door. It gave a little squeak, but not much. He silently moved down the hall toward the stairs.

Then he spotted it.

It was on the kitchen table, and it wasn't good. There, piled in humiliation, were his cables, his tape recorder, and all of his other electronic gizmos.

The jig was up.

"Nicholas?" It was Dad. He was sitting in the family room. Apparently he had heard the squeaky door. At that moment, Nick hated that door. His dad's voice was cool and collected. Too cool and collected. "Come in here," he ordered.

Nicholas swallowed hard and obeyed. Slowly, though . . . very slowly.

"Sit down."

There was no mistaking that tone of voice. That was the tone that said, "I'm not going to yell; I'm not going to holler. I'm going to deal with this in a quiet, civilized manner." In other words, Nick was going to get it, and he was going to get it good.

If that wasn't bad enough, there was Mom. She was sitting across the coffee table pretending to read her *Ladies' Home Journal.* However, by the way she was flipping through the pages, you knew she wasn't really seeing them. In fact, she wasn't really seeing anything—except red.

"Were you at the movies?" Dad asked.

For the briefest second, Nick thought about lying. He could say he heard about a gigantic traffic accident on the radio . . . that he'd run downtown to give all the victims mouth-to-mouth resuscitation and save hundreds of lives. Or he could say that, out his window, he'd seen a jet airliner lose it's wing in the air . . . he'd raced to the airport to talk the pilot down to a safe landing. Or maybe they'd believe he had suddenly found a cure for cancer and had to rush down to the hospital so not one more life would be lost.

All these thoughts flashed through his mind in a few seconds. But Nick decided the truth would be better. He'd done enough deceiving for one day.

Besides, if he told the truth, maybe they'd let him off easy. You know, something light like life imprisonment.

"Yes, sir," he answered his dad's question, barely above a whisper.

"Did you enjoy yourself?" his dad asked.

Again it was time for the truth. "No, sir . . . it was awful."

Mom and Dad exchanged looks.

Finally Mom spoke up. "Do you realize what you've done?" she asked.

Nicholas couldn't look up. He couldn't look into their eyes. He could only look at the ground.

"Son . . ." It was Dad now. "When your mother and I said you couldn't see that movie, we had a purpose."

Nick wanted to say something. He wanted to say that he understood now, that he knew their purpose. But no words came to mind. There was nothing but a tightness forming in the back of his throat. A tightness he couldn't swallow away.

"We wanted to protect you," Mom said.

"Nicholas. Look at me," Dad said quietly. "Nicholas."

It was hard, but at last the boy raised his head. He knew that what his dad was about to say was very important. He knew he'd better hear every word.

"Son," Dad continued, "your mind is the most important thing you have. That's why the Lord is so clear when he tells us to be careful what we put into it."

The boy continued to hold his dad's gaze. He would not, could not, look away.

Dad continued, "Whether you enjoyed that show or not is beside the point. By going to see it, you've allowed something to come into your mind . . . to corrupt it . . . to dirty it."

Nick knew exactly what Dad meant. Boy, did he know.

Then it was Mom's turn. "There are scenes inside you now that you'll never be able to erase," she said. Nick could tell how much this upset her by the sad tone of her voice. "Pictures that may stay with you the rest of your life."

Suddenly Nick's eyes started to burn. He wanted to say something. He wanted to let them know what he was feeling. But there were only two words that came to mind. Two words that captured what he felt about disobeying them, about deceiving them, and about seeing the movie. . . .

"I'm sorry," he whispered hoarsely.

There was a moment of silence. They knew he meant it. Finally Dad answered. "I'm sorry, too, Son." Another moment. Then Dad continued. "Now I want you to go up to your room and give this some thought. I'll be up in a little while to talk about your punishment."

Nicholas nodded slightly and rose to his feet. The movie had been awful, there was no doubt about that. What had been even more awful, though, was knowing how he'd disappointed his parents, how he'd let them down. As he turned, hot tears spilled onto his cheeks.

His back was to Mom and Dad, so they couldn't see his face . . . but it wouldn't have mattered. They were too busy fighting back the moisture in their own eyes to have seen his.

Being a kid is tough, no doubt about it. Being a parent who loves your child enough to do what's best—even when it hurts both of you—well, that's probably even tougher.

NINE
Wrapping Up

Been many a day since he's seen the sun,
got no time to play,
got no time for fun.
'Cause he's having to pay for the things he's done.
Quiet as a mouse.
When Mom and Dad said no,
snuck out to see a scary show.
That's how he found out
Ya reap what ya sow.

The following week found us reaping the "rewards" of our caper. As punishment for sneaking out of the house, Nick had to do various chores around the house.

He was in the middle of hauling a big load of boxes up to the attic when he stopped in the kitchen for a well-deserved drink. I, of course, was helping out by taking the demanding job of "Chief Supervisor in Charge of Personnel." I had positioned myself atop the kitchen table. Someone had to make sure the box hauling journey from the garage to the attic went smoothly for my young friend.

As Nick downed a second glass of water, I tightened the

straps on my work gloves and hitched up my support belt another notch. (You can never be too careful when it comes to hard physical labor.)

"Whew! I need a break," Nick said, wiping his brow and setting the glass down on the table.

"So, are we finished?" I asked.

"No, we are not finished. I still have to haul the rest of these boxes from the garage to the attic."

Despite his tone of voice, I knew Nick was really glad to have my help. He just doesn't show his feelings that much.

"Boy, the folks are riding you kind of hard, aren't they?" I commented.

"It could be worse," Nick said. "I could have to through that stupid movie again."

We both laughed. Sitting through that movie had been the most agonizing two hours of our lives (except maybe for the time we had to go to the aluminum siding and storm-door expo with Mr. Dad). Anyway, hauling boxes was a picnic by comparison.

"I tell you, McGee, I'm through watching garbage like that," Nick said. I smiled. The experiences of that last few days had really taught him a valuable lesson. "But you gotta help me," he added. "That kind of stuff is all around."

Of course, I would be glad to help my little pal. After all, it's easier to stick to your guns when you've got somebody standing beside you.

"Yeah, it's tough making the right choices," I answered. "But it's like I always told you: The road to ruin is paved with crude inventions."

Nick rolled his eyes and grinned slightly as he got up and gathered the boxes he had dumped on the kitchen table.

"Inventions!" he said, laughing. "You mean like the time you told me to use Mom's vacuum cleaner to rake the yard?"

"It would have worked if you hadn't hit the sprinkler," I said, scooping some raspberry jam out of the jar next to me.

Nick just shook his head and started hauling the boxes toward the stairs. "Or how about the time you told me to cut the sleeves off my shirt so Mom wouldn't see where I tore it? Or the time . . ." His voice trailed off in the distance as he headed up the stairs.

Sure, I remembered all those things. It was clear Nick had a great memory, too. It was clear that it could take some time to put the last few days behind us. And believe me, that movie and Nick's "escape" were things I would just as soon forget.

One thing was sure, though: Nick and I would have a lot more memories—some good, some bad. If we were smart, we'd use all of them to make the road ahead a little easier to follow. Or at least a little clearer. Knowing Nick and me, that road would be paved with fun, friendship, and above all, adventure.

Stay tuned, sports fans. . . .

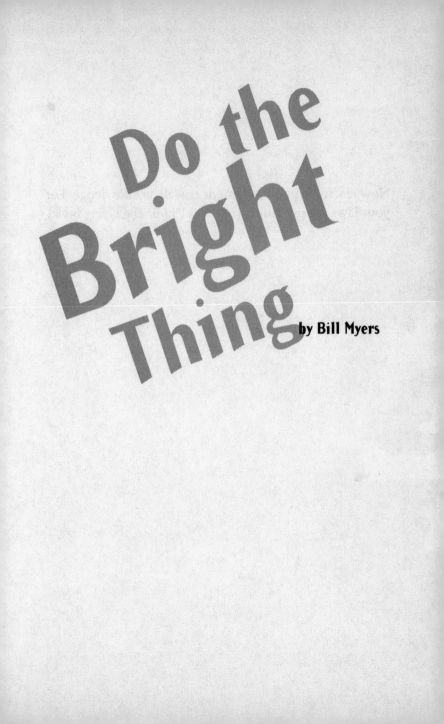

Do the Bright Thing

by Bill Myers

Now teach me good judgment as well as knowledge. For your laws are my guide. (Psalm 119:66, *The Living Bible*)

ONE
Professor Gizmo

I strapped my breathtakingly beautiful body into the Photon Combustion Accelerator and began switching switches, dialing dials, and knobbing knobs. Faster than you could say, "Oh no! What's this incurably cute and contagiously clever cartoon character concocting this time?" the Accelerator crackled to life.

Yes, it is I—Professor Pepto Gizmo—world-famous inventor and frozen yogurt connoisseur.

Now, it's true, my inventions haven't always been the success I'd hoped. Like my remote-controlled, solar-powered umbrella opener. Hey, don't laugh. It was terrific, except for the fact that it only worked when the sun was out. Then there was my fully automatic, jet-powered tooth flosser. Again, a terrific success, except that it occasionally yanked out a tooth. (The public can be so picky sometimes.)

All of that was behind me now (except for the dental bills). Now it was time to test my crowning achievement. The concept was simplistically simple. Every night for years those glitzy and glamorous TV stars had traveled on the air waves all the way across the country to my TV set, just so I could see them in my living room. It didn't seem fair. I mean, if we were such good friends, I should have to go to their homes once in a while, too.

Well! My handy-dandy Photon Accelerator would change all of that. I pushed the thrust energizers all the way forward to "Here Goes Nothin'" and grabbed the remote control to my TV. I smiled as I imagined myself landing right in the middle of all my favorite TV stars (who, of course, would be flocking around me to applaud my genius). I pressed the button. Crackle-zzzzzt-pop! I was transported into Video Land.

I looked around. Hey, wait a minute! Something was wrong! A quick glance at the remote explained it: Someone had set the channel selector to the wrong station! I wasn't surrounded by stars. Instead, I was riding the back of some bird, who was singing about the letter H and the number 9. The only thing stranger than the song was the bird—he was huge and yellow and couldn't sing on key if his life depended on it!

I leaped from his back and landed on a front porch, just in time for this blue fur ball to start chasing me all over the place screaming, "Me want cookie. . . . Me want cookie!" Hey, cookies sounded good—and normally I would have stuck around for a bite to eat—but I had this sneaking suspicion that the fur ball's "bite" was gonna be me!

I ran up the steps, only to be met by this weird guy with a Dracula-type accent. I grabbed his arm and asked, "Where am I? Where am I?" But all he did was count the number of times I asked the question.

"Dat's vun 'Vhere am I'. . . . Dat's two 'Vhere am I's,' ah-ha-ha-ha."

Suddenly I heard an argument behind me. I spun around just in time to see the letters K and O punching it out. I tell you, on a weirdness scale of one to ten, this place was definitely an eleven. It was too much, even for me. So I grabbed the remote control and pushed another channel.

Zzzzzt-pop-click!

Now where was I? Let's see. . . . There were a couple of Mom-and-Pop types standing around in a kitchen that looked like it was right out of the fifties. Come to think of it, the Mom and Pop kinda looked like they came out of the fifties, too!

Best I could figure, they were either forest rangers, or they worked at a zoo, 'cause all they did was talk about this Beaver. Everything was "the Beaver this," "the Beaver that." It's like he was practically part of the family or something. He even had his own room upstairs!

Now don't get me wrong. I'm all for animal rights and everything. But what was gonna happen when ol' Beaver boy decided to start building dams in the bathtub?

Oh, and there was one other problem. As nice as Momsie and Popsie were, there was no getting around one cold, hard fact: These folks were boring. I mean, they made memorizing multiplication tables seem like a trip to Disneyworld.

"Come on, folks!" I hollered. "How 'bout a little action, a little drama?"

They smiled at me blankly.

"Don't you guys ever argue? Don't you ever fight?"

"Ah," Mom said nodding and seeming to understand. "How about some cookies and a glass of nice warm milk? Wally will be home soon and—"

"No, no, no!" I shouted, feeling myself getting a little hot under the collar. "Action! Drama! DOESN'T ANYTHING EVER HAPPEN AROUND HERE?"

It was no use. They just didn't understand. So before they could suggest we sit at the table for a nice, long, boring talk about the problem . . .

Zzzzzt-pop-click! I hit the channel selector.

Sizzling smoke rings! I must have landed in the middle of a gigantic fire! Everywhere I looked there was smoke and smog. I mean, either I was in a gigantic fire, or I was in downtown Los Angeles.

But hold it! In front of me were a zillion screaming crazies. Each and every one was jumping up and down. They were shrieking and dancing for all they were worth (which couldn't have been more than twenty-five cents, judging from the way they looked). Apparently I'd stumbled upon some primitive Stone-Age tribe carrying out their crazed, sacrificial rituals. I figured I must have made my way into a National Geographic special. But my fancy figuring proved faulty.

Suddenly there was a tremendous explosion behind me—so loud that it knocked me to my knees. Actually, it wasn't an explosion. It was a roar. A roar that wouldn't stop. A roar that drove the natives even crazier.

I spun around just in time to see four strange and eerie creatures—aliens! I mean, these guys looked worse than E.T.!

One of the mutants was behind a control panel that looked a lot like a keyboard. Another one was behind what appeared to be a set of drums. Two others were holding strange-looking weapons disguised as guitars. But they couldn't be guitars. Guitars couldn't possibly make the awful noise these things made! They had to be some sort of living organisms that the aliens were tormenting. You could tell by their ghastly screeches and growls that the poor guitar-shaped creatures were not happy campers.

Thick, gagging smoke . . . crazed natives . . . brain-breaking blasts . . . out-of-control aliens . . . Where was I? Had I stumbled into somebody's nightmare? Had I discovered a TV station from beyond?

80

I glanced down at the channel zapper. Oh! Silly me! I'd accidentally punched up MTV!

Quicker than you could say, "Got a couple of aspirin?" I hit the road by hitting the last and final channel.

Zzzzzt-pop-click!

Ahhhh. This was more like it. Once again I was standing before a huge audience. Only this time the people were on every side. Everywhere I looked they were clapping and cheering. No one had to tell me who they were cheering for. I knew. Me, the magnificent Pepto Gizmo. Yes, at last I'd found my place—up on stage, where all my admirers could point and clap and cheer over my greatness.

Suddenly there was the clang of a bell. The lights dimmed and . . . hold it! . . . wait a minute! I wasn't on a stage. I was . . . I was in a ring—A BOXING RING!!!

And . . . wait a minute! What wise guy stole my pants? Who put me in these . . . uh-oh! Not only was I in a boxing ring, but . . . I WAS WEARING BOXING SHORTS!!!

The crowd gasped. Since I know my legs aren't that ugly, I figured that there was something coming up behind me. From the looks on people's faces, I could tell it was big and tall and probably not some Girl Scout trying to sell cookies.

I took a quick look at the remote and . . . holy heart attack! I was in an HBO Sports Special!

I quickly pressed the channel selector.

PHISSST-wop!

Nothing happened. I pressed it again.

PHISSST-wop!

And again.

PHISSsssss . . .

Great—the batteries were dead!

81

Closer and closer the footsteps came. I could tell by the way the ring shook with every step that my days of painless living were quickly coming to an end. Any second now it was going to be curtains or, even worse, venetian blinds. So I did what any world-famous inventor and cartoon character would do— I screamed for the artist.

"NICHOLAS!"

Nicholas is the guy who sketches me in all of these neat adventures. Yep. That's right. All of this has just been the imaginative doodlings of my cartoonist friend, Nicholas Martin.

"NICHOLAS, GET ME OUT OF HERE! NICHO—"

Suddenly a giant boxing glove the size of the national debt grabbed me by the neck. I knew I was a goner. I knew I was history. I knew I'd never be able to watch another Brady Bunch *sequel again. Then, just when things looked their worst, I saw it. . . .*

Nick's famous No. 2 pencil, complete with that big beautiful eraser, came into the scene. He quickly erased the boxer, the ring, even the audience.

"Where were you?!" I shouted angrily from the sketch pad. I was boiling mad. "I was about to get clobbered! And what about that rock video? My ears are still ringing! And that monster that kept thinking I was a cookie! Don't you have any consideration?! And another thing . . ."

I was really giving it to him. There was no shutting me up now. That is, until the No. 2 pencil came back onto the scene. Then, before I could finish the sentence, it had completely erased my mouth.

I was speechless. Literally.

I began shaking my fists . . . which he also erased.

I tried jumping up and down, but my feet had also taken a hike.

Needless to say, Nick had made his point. He obviously wanted me to cool down a little. Not a bad idea. I was pretty worked up. And since I didn't have that many more portions of my body left, I decided I could chill out a little. Besides, from the looks of the adventure we were about to begin, I'd need all the cool (and body parts) I could get.

So, hang on to your hats, folks. . . .

TWO
10:07 A.M.

At precisely 10:07 Saturday morning, Nicholas and Louis threw open the front door to Nick's house and headed down his porch steps.

It was one of those great autumn mornings. The type where the air is crisp enough that you can see your breath but not so cold that you have to wear that bulky coat your mom bought on sale. The type where the leaves are full of color, but they haven't fallen yet so your day can't be ruined by having to rake them. The type where if you just happen to have saved $150, you might go downtown to check out the new art tables. At least, that's what Nick was planning.

"You're crazy!" Louis said for about the hundredth time. (Good friends can get away with occasionally repeating themselves.) "You're gonna use that 150 bucks you've saved up for the last year and a half to buy . . . a drawing table!?"

"Well, I haven't made up my mind yet," Nick replied as they headed around the corner to their bikes. "But this isn't just any ol' drawing table."

"Yeah, right," Louis said, smirking. As far as he was concerned, a table was a table. I mean, what kid in his

85

right mind would spend 150 smackaroos on some dumb old table? Not when there were more important things out there crying to be bought. Like the latest Nintendo or CD . . . or let's not forget the ever-present possibility of buying your very best friend in the whole world a portable TV for his room, which, of course, he would be willing to let you watch any time you came over.

Then there was the matter of Nick's bike. Now, it's not like it was twisted, or beat up, or anything like that. Hey, the fact that somebody tried to buy it as a piece of modern art last week was probably just a coincidence. Just because it was always falling apart didn't mean it was worthless. I mean, all it needed was a little paint. And, well, OK, maybe some new handlebars, a new seat, an entirely new frame, a new chain, new wheels, and a couple of new tires. Other than that, it was in great shape.

"If you ask me," Louis offered, "a new bike would be a better deal."

"Hey," Nick answered as he picked up his bike and blew the rust off the handlebars. "This bike's a lean machine."

"Right," Louis chuckled. "Betcha can't even do a wheelie on that thing."

Nick turned to his friend. Was that a challenge he heard? If it was, he had a decision to make. A little decision, but a decision nonetheless. Quicker than you can say—

Hold it, hold it just a minute. . . . Did I hear the word decision?

What's that? Who am I? Oh, sorry. It's me again . . .

McGee. And if you ask me (which you didn't, but I'll go ahead and tell you anyway 'cause that's one of the advantages of starring in your own book), this story is getting us nowhere fast. If you want some real thrills and chills, come on up here and join me in Central Control . . . better known as Nick's brain. Yes-siree-bob, there's no place more exciting (or frightening!) than the mind of an eleven-year-old!

Careful, watch your step. Sorry the place is such a mess, but Nick's been watching a lot of Saturday morning TV lately, and it kinda trashes up the place.

All the empty shelves over to your left are where Nick will be stacking the info he gets from high school and college. The spot to the right with all these cobwebs is where he's supposed to use his logic and common sense. As you can see, the place doesn't get a lot of use.

Up ahead here, this big screen with all the knobs and switches, this is the Brain Screen Computer. From here we'll be able to see how ol' Nicky-boy makes all of his decisions. Big ones, little ones, it makes no difference. It all happens right here.

OK. Let me hop up to the terminal and type in the decision Nick has to make. What was it Louis said? Oh yeah, I've got it. . . .

CHALLENGE: BET YOU CAN'T DO A WHEELIE.

Now, let's push a few buttons here and check out the options Nicholas has to sort through. There we go. . . .

OPTION A: CAN I DO IT?

Hmm, good question. Let's take a look at the screen and see.

There's Nick climbing on his beat-up excuse for a bike. There's Nick trying to do a wheelie. And there's Nick flying through the air, failing with the full fury that only a full-blown failure can fail.

Well, so much for the first option. Let's check out the second. . . .

OPTION B: WILL I BREAK MY NECK?

My guess is, you can count on it! But let's check it out. Here we go again—there's Nick on his bike. There's Nick trying even harder to do a wheelie. Hey! This time he's got the front wheel up! And this time . . . well, this time he's crashing into the ground harder than a quarterback hit by a Seattle Seahawk tackle.

Okeydokey. That takes care of Option B. And our final option . . .

OPTION C: IF I DON'T TRY, WHAT WILL LOUIS SAY?

Hey, check out the screen. There's ol' Louis up there. Boy, from this angle his nose looks like a giant banana! Now he's leaning toward us in a big close-up—I'm talking GIANT banana—and grinning that gigantic grin of his. Let's turn up the volume and hear what he says. . . .

"What's the matter, Nick? You chicken?"

Oh yeah, you got that right, Bub. Wanna see him lay an egg?

Well, my superior smarts are telling me this choice will be an easy one. Nick's gotta say, "No way." Any second now, that decision will pop up on the ol' screen, and Nick will have to tell Louis . . . oh, here it is now. See?

DECISION: OH WELL, I MAY AS WELL TRY.

WHAT!!?? Nick, you don't know how to do this! We need more data! Quick, those of you up here with me in Central Control, strap on your safety belts! Hurry! It's going to be a wild ride. Hang on. . . . HANG ON. . . .

AAAAARRRGGGGGGHHHHHHHHH!!

Back in the real world, Nicholas was trying his best to do the wheelie. At first it didn't look like he was going to make it. He kept pulling and pulling and pulling. Then, with his last ounce of effort, he finally managed to get the front wheel off the ground.

The only problem was that it came *too* far off the ground. And it kept coming. And coming. And coming some more. Then, before he knew it, Nick was flying through the air. That's OK, though. It wasn't the flying that hurt. It was the landing that smarted—a beautiful, spread-eagle, flat-on-the-back, knock-out-your-breath . . .

O M P H H H H ! ! !

Nick lay there, not moving, for a long moment.

"Hey," Louis called as he raced to him, "You OK?"

After a second—after the world stopped spinning and the pain started coming—Nicholas finally managed to let out a groan. Then, with the greatest effort, he started to get up.

"So, what say we forget the art table," Louis said with a grin as he helped Nick to his feet. "Let's just go and find some crutches."

"Ho-ho, very funny," Nicholas mumbled as he rubbed

at the pain in his backside. "Just have the ambulance drop me off at the art store."

After another moment of rear rubbing, Nick managed to get back on his bike and carefully (make that *very* carefully) start for the store. Yup, he had definitely blown that decision. Doing the wheelie was the wrong choice. But he'd learned the right lesson: Showing off can be hazardous to your health—and your backside!

Speaking of sides, on the other side of town, Nick's big sister, Sarah, was making a decision of her own. It was Saturday, so there was only one place she could be: the mall. Just as surely as water runs downhill, as surely as little brothers are always a pain in the neck, as surely as teachers never ask the questions you study for on tests . . . if it was Saturday morning, Sarah was at the mall. It was like a tradition.

This particular day was even more than a tradition; it was a celebration! After weeks of baby-sitting and saving, Sarah finally slapped her hard-earned cash down on the counter and bought the pair of white jeans she had been eyeing for months.

These weren't just any ol' pair of white jeans. These were the primo, to-the-max, super-great-looking (complete with a sparkly handpainted rainbow) pair of white jeans.

"Wow!" Tina, her best friend, called as Sarah stepped out of the dressing room.

"Whew!" Bonnie, her second-best friend, exclaimed.

"You don't think they're too much?" Sarah asked.

"No way. Do you think they have a pair in my size?" Bonnie wondered.

Sarah threw her a look. This was pretty typical. Whenever Sarah found something that was perfect and just for herself, Bonnie would always do her best to try to copy it. But that was Bonnie—kinda pushy, often bossy, and always, *always*, used to getting her own way. Luckily for Sarah, there wasn't a pair of the white jeans even close to Bonnie's size.

After Sarah had tried the pants on, and after her friends made the appropriate oohs and ahs, it didn't take much coaxing to convince her to keep wearing them. So, for the rest of the morning, no matter where they went, Sarah couldn't help feeling that everyone was watching her. She knew it probably wasn't true, but there was always the hope that she was wrong!

Now, buying things at the mall was pretty unusual for these three. Oh, they might get a slice of pizza or a taco or something like that. But most of the time they just went to hang out together and to check out all the clothes they couldn't afford. Of course, there was one other thing they always checked out. You guessed it: BOYS.

Sarah wasn't really boy-crazy, not like Tina and Bonnie. In fact, she thought the way her friends giggled and flirted with them was kind of embarrassing. Now, don't get me wrong, Sarah had plenty of friends who were boys. Most of them were pretty neat. But to think of any of them in terms of romance . . . well, Sarah figured she'd have plenty of time for that when she got older. So standing around and watching guys . . . well, that was more for the gals in romance novels and soap operas. It just wasn't for the level-headed, clear-thinking Sarah Martins of the world.

"Hey, guys," Tina whispered. "Check it out. . . . Here comes my cousin Jason with one of his buddies."

Sarah and Bonnie glanced up from their tacos. Down the walkway came a couple of average-looking guys. At least Sarah thought they were average. Apparently, Bonnie disagreed. The fact of the matter is, she was practically choking on a piece of lettuce. "He's gorgeous!" she whispered.

"Hey, Tina, what's happenin'?" her cousin said casually as he and his friend sauntered up.

"Hi, Jas. Not much," Tina answered.

"Who are your friends?" Jason asked. He said "friends," but by the way he was checking out Sarah, it was pretty obvious he meant "friend." Sarah glanced down. She could feel her cheeks start to burn. Part of her was pleased with the attention, but part of her was also uncomfortable.

"This here's Bonnie," Tina said.

"Hi!" Bonnie croaked, still trying to swallow her lettuce.

"And Sarah," Tina added.

Sarah smiled.

Jason stared. That is, until his friend gave him a jab in the gut. "Oh, uh, and this here's uh . . . uh . . . Willard."

An uneasy silence settled over the group. But since Tina could never survive over eight and a half seconds of silence, she tried something else. "Jason here, he races stock cars . . . don't you, Jas?"

"Yeah, that's right," he said, grinning. "Got a big race tonight. You babes oughta come by and check it out."

"We'd love to!" Bonnie chirped in delight.

Tina gave her a look that would freeze the sun. A look

that said, "I know it's probably not possible, but could you maybe play it just a little bit cool?"

Jason didn't notice. He was still staring at Sarah. "Decent jeans," was all he said.

Sarah's face got hotter.

Then, turning to the rest of the group he finished, "Maybe we'll see you there." With that he gave Tina a little punch in the arm and headed off. "Take care, Cuz. . . ."

"You, too, Jas," Tina said, looking very pleased with herself. The guys were less than five feet away when the girls quickly pulled into a little circle of whispers, giggles, and laughter.

"He really likes you," Tina crowed.

"You think so?" Bonnie asked as she straightened her hair.

"Not you . . . I meant Sarah."

Sarah grinned. Now that Jason wasn't right there staring away at her, being liked suddenly felt a lot better.

"And the pants," Bonnie admitted. "He loved the pants!"

"So are you going?" Tina demanded.

"Where?" Sarah asked.

"To the races, dork-brain."

"How? I don't have any way to get—"

"No sweat," Tina interrupted. "I can get my dad to drop us off."

"I don't know . . . ," Sarah stalled.

"C'mon, it'll be great!" Bonnie added.

"How do you know your mom will let you go?" Sarah asked Bonnie.

"She's just like Tina's dad—she'll let me do anything I want," Bonnie said with confidence.

"Jason really likes you, I can tell," Tina said, giving Sarah a knowing nod. "Hey, maybe he can get us a pit pass . . . that's where the real action is during the race."

"Cool!" Bonnie exclaimed.

Sarah didn't say much. She wasn't so sure it was all that "cool." I mean, Jason was sixteen, maybe older. What would she, a little fourteen-year-old, be doing hanging around some old guy like that? Besides, what would her folks say? Oh, sure, it wasn't like an official date, or anything like that. It was just some girls going to the stock car races. Lots of kids did that. Still . . .

Sarah's thoughts began to churn. She knew she'd have to make a decision. She just wasn't too sure what that decision would be.

THREE
10:42 A.M.

Nicholas thought The Art Shop was a pretty cool place.
He was hoping Louis would think so, too. But the look
on Louis's face when they entered the store told Nick his
hopes were too high. Impressing Louis was tough.
I mean, for Louis to think something was "cool," it would
have to be extra-ultra-totally-super-cool-to-the-max for
the rest of us mortals. It wasn't that Louis was hard to
please—he was just the only kid Nick knew who had
come back from California totally bored. I mean, Louis's
idea of a time without boredom would be something like
a ride on the space shuttle . . . and then only if they had
a big-screen TV and an excellent stereo system.

Nick sighed and looked around the store. Off in the
corner, by itself, was the art table he had been talking
about. As he had pointed out, this wasn't just any old art
table. It was definitely the Super-Deluxe-with-Everything-
You-Need-and-Then-Some Model. This puppy was so
high tech, it looked like it came right off the Starship
Enterprise.

Nick slowly walked toward it. He gently rubbed his
hand over the chrome-and-glass borders. In awe, he
touched the sleek pen and pencil tray. Next he tried out

the ultra-high-tech lamp. Even the art file drawer looked like something Mr. Sulu should be using to "lock on coordinates."

He turned to Louis with a look of triumph. He didn't have to say a word. It should be obvious that this was no ordinary table. Any minute now Louis would be apologizing for all the put-downs he'd made about the cost of the table. Any minute now he'd nod his head saying, "You're right, Nick, this table is awesome." Any minute now . . .

"This is 150 bucks?!" Louis crowed. "Does this thing do your homework, too?"

Nicholas closed his eyes. Sometimes he hated reality. But before he had a chance to respond to Louis, an answer came from around the corner.

"Not quite," a cheery voice remarked. "But it does get over twenty-five miles per gallon."

The kids looked up just as Graham Boatwright, the store owner, joined them. He was a jolly, well-fed fellow. It wouldn't be fair to say he's fat, but there was no mistaking the fact that he hadn't missed a meal in a while . . . quite a while. Come to think of it, he didn't miss too many in-between-meal meals, either.

"Hi, Graham," Nick said with a grin.

"What d'ya say, Nick?" Graham asked as he ran his hand over the sleek surface. "Ain't she a beaut?"

Nick had to nod.

"'Course I can't guarantee it'll make you draw any better."

"I know," Nick agreed. "But maybe using a table like this would, you know . . . inspire me."

"Hey, c'mon. That's what sunsets are for."

The two exchanged smiles.

Louis started looking around. It's not like he was bored or anything like that. But if they happened to catch some action, like getting hit by a good earthquake or hurricane right now, you wouldn't hear him complaining.

"I know what you mean about inspiration," Graham continued. "In art school they used to tell us, 'You're only as good as your tools.'"

"Really?" Nick asked. "So what did you do?"

"I went out and bought a new wrench-and-socket set!"

The two broke out laughing.

Louis figured this was artist-type humor, 'cause it sure didn't do anything for him. The best he could do was roll his eyes.

"OK . . . ," Graham chuckled. "Enough comedy."

"So that's what it was," Louis muttered.

Fortunately Graham didn't hear him. "Now, back to the sales pitch. What do your parents think?"

"Well . . . ," Nick hesitated. "I don't think they're against it, but I'm not really sure they know all the details."

"Like maybe you're nuts!" Louis cracked.

Graham gave a little smile. He found Louis's humor about as funny as Louis found his. "Look," he said turning back to Nick. "Why not have one final sit-down and talk it over with your folks." Then he added with a grin, "Have you tried holding your breath till they agree to pay for half?"

Nick chuckled. "No . . . the last time Jamie, my little sister, tried that, my dad said she looked better in purple."

Again the two guys laughed. Louis barely heard them. He was busy hoping that the rumble of that passing truck outside was a jet liner coming in for a crash landing. Maybe that would liven up the party.

No such luck.

"Well," Graham finally finished. "I don't want to rush you, but this is the last one I've got in stock. I'm afraid you're going to have to make up your mind pretty soon."

Nick nodded. It was a tough decision, no doubt about it. And he didn't have much time to make it. But right now it was time for another decision. One for which Louis would be eternally grateful. . . .

It was time to leave the art store.

Meanwhile, on the drive home from the mall, Tina was forcing someone else to make a decision.

"Daddy?" Tina's voice had a smooth, slow drawl to it.

Sarah turned from the car window to look at her friend. She knew Tina had come from the South. But she'd never heard her use this thick an accent before.

"What's up, sugar?" her father asked. Tina's mother was supposed to have picked them up. But since her dad was in the area, he had decided to swing on by.

"Well, me an' the girls here . . ." Tina curled up closer to her father. "We was kinda hopin' ta watch Jason do some racin' at the stock-car rally tonight."

Sarah watched with interest. With every word Tina's voice seemed to get warmer and softer. The girl was really pouring it on. In fact, if her voice got any sweeter, she was going to give everyone in the car a toothache. But her father didn't seem to notice.

"An' we was wonderin' if you'd like ta take little ol' me an' my friends over there later on." By now she was actually resting her head on his shoulder.

"Oh, I'm sorry, darlin'," he answered. And you could tell by the tone in his voice that he really was. "But I promised ta take Jimmy an' his friends ta the cinema."

"Well, that just figures," Tina scorned. Suddenly her warm southern voice had an icy northern chill.

Sarah continued to watch. She had heard that Tina could get anything she wanted from her folks. Now, for the first time, she had the chance to watch the "expert" in action.

But nothing happened. In fact, for several moments they just rode in silence. What was wrong? Had Tina given up—just like that? Sarah continued to watch. Then she saw it. Tina's dad was starting to fidget. Soon, he was actually beginning to throw nervous glances in his daughter's direction.

Tina said nothing.

He cleared his throat.

She still said nothing. By now it was becoming obvious that Tina was giving her dad the silent treatment. And it was pretty obvious it was starting to do the trick.

"I hope ya undastand, cupcake," Tina's dad said apologetically.

"I 'undastand' plenty." Tina scowled as she folded her arms and looked out the window.

"Now, darlin', what's that supposed ta mean?"

"It just means that whenever Jimmie wants to go somewhere, he goes. But I ask fer one litta favor, an' ya'd a thought I'd asked fer the moon."

"Now, honey, ya know that ain't so."

"Is too."

"Sugar—"

"Is too, an' you know it!"

Sarah caught her breath. If she talked back to her dad like that, she'd be lucky to get out of the house for a year. But not Tina. She had her father exactly where she wanted him.

"Listen . . . I have an idea," he said. "What say I swing by an' get us all some pizza. Maybe yer friends can stay over an'—"

"No, thank ya. I am not interested," Tina said coldly.

Sarah marveled. Tina's father was making a peace offering, but the girl would have none of it. She was obviously holding out for a higher offer. Yes sir, she was a pro. No doubt about it.

More silence.

Again Tina's father shifted uncomfortably. If there was one thing he didn't like it was not being liked . . . especially by his "darlin'" daughter.

"Sugar?"

More silence.

"Sugar, come on now an' talk ta me."

Still more silence.

Then it finally happened. He broke. The poor man just could not bear being shut out. "Well, what say we try this?" he offered. "Why don't I drop you an' yer little friends off at tha races then go on over an' take Jimmy to the cinema. How's that sound?"

"I'm afraid it'd jus' be too much trouble for ya," Tina answered, her voice still stiff and cool.

Again Sarah smiled. This girl knew all the tricks.

100

"No," her father insisted. "It wouldn't be that much trouble. It would work out jus' fine that-a-way."

"I jus' don't know. . . ."

Boy, talk about playing hard to get! The amazing thing was, it was working.

"Please, darlin', it would be my pleasure."

"Well . . ." Tina pretended to hesitate. Her dad was definitely feeling the pressure. Finally, in desperation, he had one last thought. The thought Tina had been waiting for him to come up with all along.

"Tell ya what," he said triumphantly. "If you let me take ya, I bet I'd even be willin' ta pay fer yer admission. What da ya say ta that?"

"Would ya?" Once again Tina's voice was getting that southern warmth to it. "Would ya really?"

"Of course," he said. "And fer all your friends, too." He broke into a confident smile. Boy howdy, nobody could say he didn't know how to handle his little girl. Yep, he was a reg'lar child-rearin' genius.

"Oh, thank ya, Daddy," Tina said, beaming.

"Well, I reckon it's the least I can do, don't you?"

"Oh, Daddy," she said as she curled up next to him again. "You're so good ta me."

"I know, darlin' girl," he said, putting his arm around her. "But I jus' wouldn't have it any other way."

Sarah looked on, her mouth hanging open. Tina glanced up and gave her a little wink. Yes sir, everything had worked out exactly as she had planned.

Outside the art store, Louis and Nick were getting on their bikes. Suddenly Louis had a brainstorm. "Hey, I know just what you need to relax the ol' brain cells. Let's go over to Riley's Arcade and zap some aliens!"

Nick glanced over to his friend. It was true, unwinding with some video games might help him relax and make up his mind. But if he decided to do that, it would—

Now hold it, hold it just a minute! Did my ever-so-perfect hearing hear the word it thought it heard? Did somebody decide it was time to decide another decision?

Well, come on down . . . er, up, or wherever this Brain Screen thing is, and let's take a look at ol' Nicky-boy's thoughts.

First, let me type in the question.

SHOULD I PLAY VIDEO GAMES?

Now for the options. . . .

OPTION A: IS THIS GOOD FOR ME?

Hmmm. Let's see what comes up on the screen. Hey, there's the video arcade. Oh, and here's Nick at the Trash the Mutant Blood-Sucking Pigs from Venus game. It's his favorite. Uh-oh, wait a minute. Take a look at those eyes. He must have been here all afternoon. And that frizzled hair. Looks like he's been going to Albert Einstein's barber. Talk about bushed. I mean, if this guy was any more burned out, he'd be a pile of ashes.

Oh, look, here comes good ol' Louis. Look at that, he's got the same beat-up expression. Hold on, he's about to say something important. . . .

"Got any more quarters?"

Boy, talk about the living dead. The guy sounds like he's half-asleep.

"I'm flat broke."

That was Nicholas—and he is asleep.

Well, that takes care of Option A. The arcade is about as good for Nick as going skinny-dipping in the middle of December . . . in Alaska . . . under the ice. OK, so let's see what's next on the list.

OPTION B: WHAT DO MY FOLKS SAY?

And up on the screen we see . . . oh, it's Mom. She's pointing to a watch that's strapped to her wrist that's the size of Roseanne Barr's mouth. What's she saying?

"Remember, be home by noon."

Let's see. It's fifteen minutes to noon now, and it takes fifteen minutes to get home. Hmmm . . . Looks like it's time to get out the old calculator. Ah, here we go. Now, we just add the seven, carry the three, find the square root of 3.14, divide that by its common denominator, multiply it by $E=MC^2$, throw in a pinch of salt and two cloves of garlic, click your heels together three times, and we get . . .

Well, I'm not sure what we get. (Math was never one of my strong suits.) But whatever we get, it's a safe guess those Blood-Sucking Pigs from Venus are safe for another day.

All rightee, and our last option in the old process:

OPTION C: WHAT DOES THE WISE MAN SAY?

The Wise Man, huh? I wonder who . . . ? Hey, will you take a look at that? Here comes some old geezer in robes and a long, flowing beard. Look at all those books he's carrying. This guy must really be wise—I mean, to be readin' all of those books. Either that, or he's heading up some paper drive. Hold it. He's pointing to a book on his lap. What's he saying?

"The Scripture says, 'Honor your father and mother.'"

No argument there, Grandpa. But wait a sec. Doesn't this guy look kinda suspicious? Those eyes . . . that mouth. I mean, if it wasn't for the beard, he'd look like— Hold the phone, Fred! He's pullin' down the beard. It's a fake!

That's . . . that's Nick's dad under there! Now it looks like he wants to say something else. Let's see if he has any other precious pearls of wisdom to share. . . .

"Nicholas! Did you mow the lawn yet?"

Now, that's more like it. Yes-siree, disguise 'em all you want, but no matter what you do, dads just can't stop being dads.

So where was I? Oh yeah. Let's press the ol' button here and get Nick's final decision.

There he is, back in front of the art shop. Let's listen to his conclusion:

"No way, Louis. An hour in there, and I won't have enough money to buy a pencil, much less an art table. Besides, I'm supposed to be home by noon."

Well, what do you know. He got one right. Nice work, Nick.

There they go, hopping on their bikes and merrily pedaling down the street.

Ahhh . . . I just love happy endings, don't you?

FOUR
11:59 A.M.

It was exactly 11:59 A.M. Not only had Nicholas made it home on time, but he actually had a minute to spare! Imagine being home early! What a concept! If he kept that up, he'd be giving the rest of kidhood a bad name!

He plopped down at the table just in time to see the old standby lunch (tomato soup and a grilled cheese sandwich) shoved under his face. Luckily, he managed to grab a handful of chips before they disappeared forever into the Forbidden Zone—better known as Sarah's side of the table.

Sarah wasn't saying much. She never did. That is unless she had a juicy putdown, wisecrack, or complaint—which, come to think of it, happened to be most of the time. But that should go without saying. After all, she *was* the older sister. I mean, she did have her end of the relationship to keep up.

Today, though, she said nothing. Maybe she was trying to be polite. Or maybe she finally realized it was time to start treating Nick with some respect. Yeah, well, I wouldn't bet on it. Actually, Sarah's silence had nothing to do with Nick. It had a lot to do with the fight she had just had with Mom. . . .

"But why can't I go?" she had asked.

"Sarah," her mother had sighed for the hundredth time. "You're only fourteen, and—"

"Almost fifteen," Sarah had interrupted. "I'm closer to fifteen than fourteen."

"Fine. The point is we agreed that you wouldn't start dating until you were—"

"But this isn't a date! I'm just going to the stock car races with Tina."

"To see some older boy we haven't even met!" Mom had felt her voice getting a little sharp. She hated it when that happened, yet, somehow, Sarah always knew how to get it to happen.

"But I'm not going to see *him*," Sarah had insisted. "He's just getting us some pit passes so we can go down into—"

"You're going into the pit area!?"

"Well, yeah. Tina says that's where all the action—"

"That's where all the cars zoom in and out!"

Sarah stared at the table and bit her lip. She'd blown it, no doubt. With one slip of the tongue she had cut off all possibility of going. Now, not only was Mom thinking she had a serious case on some older grease monkey, she was also picturing Sarah standing in the middle of some racetrack dodging cars all night.

It was useless. Sarah knew it. Still, she had one weapon left. A weapon she'd seen Tina use on her dad with the greatest of success. Now it was Sarah's turn to try it. . . .

Sarah sulked. She would not say another word.

For a beginner, she did a pretty good job of it. That is, until Nick barged in and brought up the topic of the art

106

table. Then . . . well, it was like she couldn't help herself. It was like her older-sister genes suddenly took over.

"Have you considered investing in something really worthwhile?" she snapped. "Like clothes?"

Now it's true, she had a point. I mean, Nick's idea of fashion was throwing on the first things he grabbed in the morning. It made little difference what color they were or even if they matched. If they were the first things his hand fumbled for, they were the first things he wore.

"Cholfes?" Nick mumbled through a mouthful of grilled cheese sandwich. "I mont to be an artist, mot a model."

"No danger in that," Sarah agreed.

"You look fine," Mom said as she handed him a glass of milk. It wasn't really the truth. But, after all, moms are expected to say that sort of thing. It's in their contract.

"Thanks," Nick answered. "So when can I talk to you and Dad about the art table? There's only one left, and I gotta make a decision by Monday."

"Your father ought to be home soon. Let's talk it over after dinner." Suddenly a thought came to her mind. A thought that only a motherly mind can think. If Nick had been paying attention, he would have seen it coming. He would have been able to make his escape ahead of time. But it was too late now.

"Hey," she asked, "speaking of Monday, don't you have a book report due?"

Nick was trapped. "Well, yeah," he said as he picked up his sandwich and started for the family room. Maybe he could still get away. "I'm almost done. I'll finish it right after *Sci-Fi Theat—*"

107

He never finished the sentence. Mom knew exactly what he was getting at and exactly how to put a stop to it. "No way," she insisted. "You were at the art store all morning. With church tomorrow you won't have time."

"Oh, Mom. . . ." But Nick knew there was no changing her mind.

"Finish the report, and then we'll see about *Sci-Fi Theater*," she said as she put the milk back in the fridge. "But I really doubt you'll have time to—" She looked back toward him and came to a stop.

Nick had already taken off for his room. There wasn't much time. But if there was any way of getting that book read before seeing *Sci-Fi Theater* . . . he'd do it.

Mom couldn't help breaking into a smile. Well, there was one thing you could say about Nick—he was determined. She looked over at Sarah, who was once again chewing her sandwich in silence. Of course, you could say the same thing about Sarah, too. . . .

Up in his room, Nick was plowing though *Treasure Island*. He was reading the sentences as fast as his little eyeballs could move. Of course, he couldn't remember half of what he was reading, but at least he was reading.

Suddenly a sickening thought came to his mind. He reached for the back of the book and started flipping the pages.

"Oh, great," he sighed. "I've still got two more chapters to read. This will take forever. Unless . . ." You could see the wheels starting to turn in his mind. "Unless I just read the last couple of pages and—"

108

Uh-oh . . . Here we go again. Time for Nicholas to make another decision. But this time it's a little more tricky. Not only does it deal with using bad judgment, like the daredevil wheelie, but it is a question of choosing between right and wrong. Let's type in the question and take a look at the data.

QUESTION: SHOULD I GIVE A REPORT ON A BOOK I HAVEN'T FINISHED READING?

The options to consider:
OPTION A: "IS IT RIGHT?"
And up on the screen we have . . . Oh, it's our favorite blue-eyed bully, Derrick Cryder. My, my, he looks especially frightening today, dressed in his favorite leather coat and brass knuckles. Looks like he'll be convincing a few more munchkins that they won't be needing their lunch money. Wait a minute, he's about to say something to Nick. Let's listen and see what cunning words our conniving con has to convey.

"Look stupid, everybody does it. Man, I just read the inside cover."

Well, thanks for sharing, Derrick. At least we have our answer about right or wrong. Now on to . . .

OPTION B: WHAT WOULD THE OTHER KIDS SAY IF THEY FOUND OUT?

Hey, there's Renee and Louis with Nicholas up on the screen. Gee, they don't look so hot. What's the matter? They got the flu? Renee's doing the talking (so, what else is new?). Let's listen. . . .

"Gee, Nick. We thought you were different when it came to being honest and stuff."

109

Not good, Nicky-roo. Not good at all. So let's go on to the next option. . . .

OPTION C: WHY DO I WANT TO DO THIS?

And here we have Nick sitting in front of the ol' tube. Let's take a peek at what he's watching.

Oh great, it's one of those Japanese sci-fi flicks. You know the type . . . with all those fakey monsters strolling through fakey models that are supposed to be real buildings. Then, of course, there's the cornball music. And let's not forget the screaming—there has to be lots and lots of screaming . . . and it must never match actors' lip movements.

There he is now. There's your average run-of-the-mill monster rising out of your average run-of-the-mill ocean about to attack your average run-of-the-mill city.

Now he's knocking over buildings, swatting down toy planes, trouncing on Match Box cars, and flossing his teeth with those ever-popular sparking power lines.

Yes-siree-bob. I tell you, Nick, this stuff is really classic. The type of thing I'd love to be cheating on book reports and ruining my reputation over.

Well, enough of that. Let's take a look at our final option. . . .

OPTION D: WHAT DOES THE WISE MAN SAY?

Ah, yes, and there's . . . wait a minute, it's dorkey Derrick again. Hey, I said wise "man," not wise "guy." Here, let me just give this screen a little kick like they taught us in computer repair school. . . .

K-THWACK!

There, that's better. Now we have the old geezer (alias Dad) speaking again.

"And the Scriptures say, 'Give me understanding that I may obey your law. . . .'"

Ah, yes, "obedience." Not always a popular word, but definitely one worth keeping around.

Well, now that we've got all of our data, let's press the old decision button here and see what comes up.

DECISION: I WANTED TO READ THE WHOLE BOOK ANYWAY.

Atta boy, Nicholas! I knew you could do it! You're two for three in the decision department! But hang on! It's going to start getting crazy. . . .

FIVE
6:30 P.M.

It was Saturday night, and Sarah had just hung up the phone. She wasn't sure why or how it had happened—but somehow Tina had managed to convince her to go to the races.

"It will be perfectly safe," Tina had said. "Daddy will be with the three of us the whole time."

"Yeah, but . . ."

"Besides, it's time they quit treating you like a little girl. I mean, you're practically fifteen. Almost a woman."

"Yeah, but . . ."

"Just tell them you're going over to my—no, you better make that Bonnie's house. Just tell them you're going to Bonnie's. . . ."

"Yeah, but . . ."

"It won't be a lie. I mean, you *will* be going there first. It won't be your fault that Daddy and I just happen to swing by and ask you to come along."

No doubt about it, Tina had a devious mind. And she wasn't afraid to use that mind on Sarah. Over and over again she had argued and reasoned . . . until Sarah finally had crumbled. *Really*, she thought as she hung up the phone, *I had no choice. I had to say yes.* Either that or, as

Tina so clearly pointed out, "You'll just be a total loser for the rest of your life."

But if everything Tina had said was so logical and made such perfect sense, how come Sarah felt so bad? I mean, she barely had the receiver back in its cradle before the waves of guilt began to wash over her.

Still, she had made her decision. Now all she had to do was live with it.

Meanwhile, over in the family room, Nick was still working on his decision. "It's really neat," he was saying to his folks. "I mean, it's got an art file drawer attached to keep my McGee drawings and stuff . . . and a tray for pencils . . . and it looks great . . . and . . . and . . . ."

Suddenly Nicholas came to a stop. If it was such a great deal, how come he was working so hard to convince his parents? Maybe it really wasn't his parents he was trying to convince. Maybe he was still trying to convince himself.

"It sounds wonderful, Son," Dad finally offered.

"But, honey . . ." It was Mom. Just as he'd always be "Son" to his dad, he'd always be "honey" to his mom. "Honey," she continued, "what's wrong with your old art table?"

"Well . . ." Nick's mind was searching desperately. "It's old! I mean, I've had it ever since . . . ever since I was a kid."

There was no missing the brief smiles that appeared on his parents' lips.

At last Dad cleared his throat and got very serious. There was no mistaking it, the verdict was about to be handed down. "Son . . . we know you've saved this money for a long time."

114

You're right about that. But what about the decision?

Dad continued. "You worked for it . . . you earned it . . . and . . ."

Yeah, yeah, go on, go on.

"And if you're certain you want to spend it on a new art table . . ."

Nick held his breath.

"Well, that's OK with us."

ALL RIGHT! HE SCORES! A BIG T.D. FOR THE KID!

Well, at least that's what Nick figured he should have thought. But something was wrong. Even with his parents' permission, something still wasn't right.

Mom was the first to notice. "So, what's the problem, honey?"

"I don't know . . . I thought if you guys said OK, that would be it. But . . ." he hesitated for a second. "I still don't really know what to do."

Mom and Dad exchanged glances. Finally Dad spoke.

"I know how you feel, Nick. And I think you're using the right approach. I mean, it seems like you've given this decision a lot of thought, and you've come to us for advice. That's great. But there's still one thing left you have to do."

"What's that?" Nick asked.

"Pray."

Nicholas looked at his father. As usual, the man was right on the button. Coming to his parents for advice was good, but now they were turning the decision back to him. Now *he'd* have to make it. And if he really wanted to make the right decision, he'd have to get one other opinion: God's.

Nick sighed. Turning to Mom and Dad for a quick yes

or no was an easy solution—sometimes too easy. But turning to the Lord and asking for his wisdom . . . well, that was a little different. It wasn't necessarily harder, but it was different. And it was a difference he'd have to get used to the older he got. . . .

Try as she might, Sarah couldn't get rid of the knot growing in her stomach. It was there when she asked Mom if she could go to Bonnie's house. (She half wished Mom would say no, but she didn't.)

It was a little bigger as she put on her new white jeans, threw on a coat, and headed out the front door.

It was a lot bigger when Tina and her dad arrived at Bonnie's to pick them up.

And it was about the size of a watermelon as they rode in the station wagon toward the races. The fact that Tina's little brother and all his friends were bouncing up and down on the seats and throwing Gummi Bears at each other didn't help much. The fact that Tina had the radio cranked up full volume helped even less.

"You girls have a good time!" her dad hollered as they pulled into the parking lot.

"Yes, Daddy," Tina shouted.

"You bet," Bonnie yelled.

Sarah didn't answer. She figured no one could hear her from the backseat anyway.

By now the car had stopped and the girls were piling out. Sarah noticed something green and gooey sticking to her new white jeans—a lime Gummi Bear (half-chewed, of course) had found a permanent home on her right leg. *Oh great,* she thought as she bent over and started picking it off.

"The movie gets out at 9:30," Tina's dad yelled as he began pulling away. "We'll be by ta pick ya up 'bout a quarter ta ten."

"Thank ya, Daddy!" Tina called.

He gave a wave and was gone.

Suddenly Sarah looked up. "Wait a minute. . . . Wait a minute! Where's your dad going?"

"Taking my brother and his scum-bucket friends to the movies."

"But . . . didn't you say he'd be with us?" Sarah tried to be cool, but there was no missing the concern in her voice.

"Did I?" Tina asked innocently. "Oh, well, he'll be back in a couple of hours."

Sarah wasn't thrilled, and she made no effort to hide it.

"Come on," Bonnie chided, "don't be such a prude. It's only a couple of hours. What trouble can we get into in just two hours?"

"Oh, I bet we'll find something," Tina giggled.

"Let's hope so," Bonnie giggled back. "Come on, let's go!"

"But guys . . . ," Sarah called. "Guys!"

It did no good. Her two friends were already halfway across the parking lot. Not wanting to be left alone, Sarah let out a sigh and followed them . . . all the time, of course, picking at the gooey green gunk stuck to her leg.

Back at home, Nicholas was up in his room. He wasn't reading. He wasn't inventing one of his neat inventions. He wasn't even drawing a McGee adventure.

He was making out a list. A decision list. On one side were all of the reasons to buy the art table. On the other side were all of the reasons not to buy. But things weren't going the way he'd hoped. It seemed he had more than enough reasons for the "Not to Buy" column and only a couple for the "Buy" column. He tried to even them out, but pretty soon the whole thing was looking a little lopsided:

DECISION LIST

Reasons to Buy	Reasons NOT to Buy
It would keep me organized.	It costs too much.
It would be fun.	Could buy lots of other things.
It would be fun.	Could save for new bike.
It would be fun.	Don't really need it.
It would be fun.	Use money to help others.
It would be fun.	Could save for college.

After a moment, Nick crumpled the paper and tossed it into the trash. This definitely was not going the way he wanted.

"Isn't this great?"

"WHAT?"

"I SAID, ISN'T THIS GREAT!"

The roar of the stock cars was too loud. Sarah had to read Bonnie's lips to figure out what she was saying.

"YES," Sarah finally shouted back. "BUT ARE YOU SURE WE'RE SUPPOSED TO BE HERE??"

"WHAT?" Bonnie shouted.

"WE'RE NOT SIXTEEN—THE SIGN SAID YOU HAVE TO BE SIXTEEN TO BE IN THE PITS!"

118

"WE GOT THE PASSES, DIDN'T WE?"

"YEAH, BUT—"

"WHAT??"

Sarah just shook her head. She'd been called a prude once tonight. Once was enough. If they weren't supposed to be there, well, let Tina's cousin, Jason, get in trouble. After all, he was the one who got them the passes.

To be honest, Sarah was a little disappointed in Jason's reaction when he saw her. She wasn't expecting him to do handsprings. But she was expecting more than a quick "Hi" before he began yelling at his partner to fix the distributor or carburetor or whatever it was.

Obviously he didn't know what she had gone through to get there—the lying, the sneaking, the knot in her gut . . . and now the permanent loss of hearing.

But that was half an hour ago. Now Jason was out on the track with half a dozen other cars. Now they were all fighting for position as they waited for the starting flag and the beginning of the race.

Tina and Bonnie were practically glowing with excitement. I mean, here they were, right in the heart of the action. Everywhere they looked people were running, sweating, swearing, smelling of gas, borrowing tools, desperately trying to fix their cars for their upcoming heats. And here they were, three kids, standing right in the middle of it.

"There they go!" Tina shouted.

All heads turned back to the track just in time to watch the cars get the green flag and start the race.

Suddenly everyone was going full throttle . . . fighting for position . . . gunning . . . braking . . . trying to squeeze

119

past one another. Anything went—and that's what they tried: anything.

The noise was deafening. The smell of exhaust was suffocating.

Around and around the track they roared, always staying in a tight pack. Each time they thundered past the pit, the girls could feel the wind from the cars against their faces.

And then it happened. . . .

The second-place car, a yellow one, made its move and somehow forced the lead car against the wall. The car didn't hit the wall hard, just hard enough to lose a wheel . . . which bounced out into the middle of the track! A green car hit the tire and began spinning, which sent a red car sliding . . . and careening right into Jason's front side!

"Oh, my gosh!" Tina screamed.

"He's been hit!" Bonnie cried.

The three girls watched in horror as Jason fought for control. First he swerved to the right, then to the left. Somehow he managed to hang on until, at last, he spun out into the pit area. There was dust and smoke everywhere. And most of the smoke was coming from Jason's car!

"Looks like a fire!" somebody yelled. Immediately half a dozen men raced toward the car—many with fire extinguishers.

"Jason! Jason!!" Tina screamed as she started running toward his car. It was more than five hundred feet away and already surrounded by people, but there was no stopping her.

"Tina!" Bonnie shouted. "Tina, come back!!" She

120

started after her friend. Sarah also shouted and was about to follow. But then she saw it. . . .

The green car, which had spun out, was now bouncing into the pit area.

And heading right for Bonnie!

"Bonnie, look out!" Sarah shouted. But no one heard.

Suddenly, everything became a slow-motion movie. . . .

The car swerved hard to the right to try to miss Bonnie. Catching the movement out of the corner of her eye, Bonnie turned to see the car. The front end had managed to miss her, but the rear end was sliding directly toward her. She opened her mouth to scream, but she didn't have time. She tried to jump out of the way, but she was too late.

Sarah felt paralyzed as she watched the rear fender catch Bonnie on the leg, and send her flying through the air.

"BONNIE!" Even Sarah's scream sounded as if it was in slow motion as she watched her friend sail through the air. Finally Bonnie hit the ground—hard . . . too hard.

Sarah tore after her, her feet flying across the ground.

"BONNIE!" But no one heard. No one saw. Everybody was still paying attention to Jason—pulling him out of his smoking car—putting out the fire in his engine. "BONNIE!!"

Bonnie wasn't answering. She wasn't raising her head and looking around with that silly grin she always wore when she did something stupid. She wasn't moving . . . at all. She just lay on the ground like some limp, broken doll.

Sarah reached her friend and dropped to her knees. The

ground was soaked in water and oil. She could feel the cold dampness as it soaked through her pants.

"Bonnie . . . Bonnie . . . ," Sarah said in a trembling voice. But there was no answer. Sarah scooped her hands under Bonnie's head, and felt something wet and sticky on her fingers. Blood. Bonnie was bleeding. Not a lot, but enough.

"Somebody help us!" Sarah cried. "Somebody please help us!"

The driver of the green car had leaped out and was racing toward them. Now other people had noticed and were starting to follow.

Sarah was cradling Bonnie's bleeding head on her lap. She was rocking her, ever so slightly, back and forth, back and forth . . . and she was sobbing.

"Somebody help us!" Her voice was so choked the words came out in a whisper. The tears were flowing, and they wouldn't stop. "Somebody . . . please help us. . . ."

SIX
10:30 P.M.

Sarah sat in the hospital waiting room. She didn't know how long she'd been there, but if it had been a couple of minutes past forever, she wouldn't have been surprised.

Back at the racetrack, it had been a nightmare: people running, the ambulance zooming up, paramedics shouting orders. All of this as the driver of the green car kept yelling, "I didn't see her. . . . I just didn't see her!"

The paramedics had moved in and gently pried Sarah away from Bonnie. At first Sarah wouldn't let go, but their calm coaxing finally had convinced her there was nothing more she could do. After all, they were the experts. It was up to them now.

Before Sarah knew it, she had been eased back into the group of spectators. Suddenly she was just part of the crowd, jostling and craning her neck like all the others just to get a peek at what was happening to her friend.

She hadn't been able to see much. Being five-foot-two had its disadvantages. She had only caught occasional glimpses of the paramedics hovering over Bonnie. It had looked like they had attached some sort of tubing to her arm. Then they'd turned around and pulled a collapsible gurney out of the ambulance.

Sarah had gotten another glance of them carefully slipping a board under Bonnie and strapping her to it. Then, in one quick movement, they had hoisted her up, laid her on the gurney, and wheeled her toward the ambulance.

Sarah remembered how the flashing red and orange lights had hurt her eyes—but she'd continued to watch. The first attendant had hopped inside with Bonnie while the other slammed the doors and raced around to the front.

Then they were off. Just like that. Just like that, her friend was gone. Just like that, she felt all alone and deserted. But there was one thing that made her feel a little better. Not enough to smile, but enough to ease the pain . . . a little.

As they were wheeling Bonnie toward the ambulance Sarah caught a glimpse of her face. Her eyes were open. They were scared, looking all around, and filled with tears. But at least they were open.

That had been almost an hour and a half ago. Since then, Tina's dad had picked them up and they were all waiting in the hospital. Tina, her dad, Jason, Bonnie's mom, the driver of the green car, and Sarah.

But two more people were about to arrive. Sarah's parents suddenly appeared in the doorway. They were not smiling.

"Mom! Dad!" Sarah was up on her feet and in Mom's arms before she knew it. She buried her face deep into Mom's coat. She hadn't done that since she was a kid, but she was doing it now. It was like she wanted to stay buried in there forever—never wanting to leave that comfort and safety again.

124

She wasn't sure why, but she was crying . . . sobbing. And to be honest, Mom was fighting back tears of her own.

"Sweetheart, are you all right?" Dad asked her, his voice a little unsteady. But she couldn't answer—she was still sobbing into Mom's coat. "Sweetheart?" he repeated, his voice growing more concerned. "Sweetheart?"

At last Sarah was able to look up. "Oh, Daddy . . . ," she sobbed, then she threw her arms around him.

"Honey," Mom said, brushing away her own tears. "We were so worried. . . . It could have been you who was hurt."

All Sarah could do was nod as she hung on to both of them. The teenager in her knew she should be embarrassed acting this way in public, in front of Tina and Jason and everyone. But right now she didn't care. Right now she wanted to keep holding on to them and never let go.

Mom and Dad exchanged glances. They had been pretty angry when they got the phone call—when they learned that Sarah had disobeyed and deceived them. All the way over in the car, Dad kept saying how upset and disappointed he was . . . and what type of discipline Sarah would have to face.

Right now, though, wasn't a time for discipline. He knew that. It was a time for love. Oh, make no mistake about it—the discipline would come, and it would come hard. But right now it was time to hold, and hug, and even cry a little.

A few minutes later, the doctor entered. Suddenly everything got very quiet.

"Mrs. Putnam?" he said, looking at the group gathered there.

"Yes," Bonnie's mom said, as she nervously stepped forward. Sarah's folks stood right beside her in case the news was bad.

"Your daughter's going to be fine," the doctor told her.

You could hear a sigh of relief all around the room.

"She has a mild concussion," the doctor continued, "and a fractured left leg. There's nothing to worry about, but we would like to keep her at the hospital overnight for observation."

"Can I see her?" Mrs. Putnam asked.

"Certainly. Would you care to follow me?"

Bonnie's mom nodded as they quickly moved out of the room and down the hall toward her daughter's room.

Sarah wanted to see Bonnie, too, but she knew this wasn't the time. This was a time just for mother and daughter. Besides, there were other matters that Sarah had to attend to . . . like her own mother and father. It wasn't going to be pleasant, but it had to be done.

Meanwhile, back at home, Nicholas and McGee were facing their own unpleasantness. . . .

The dastardly dinosaurs were drooling all over their delectable delicacy . . . me—Caveman McGee! We'd been playing a pretty intense game of "Run for Your Life or We'll Gobble You Up!" Now that they had me cornered, it looked like I was it . . . in more ways than one.

Suddenly I started to really hate this game.

Now don't get me wrong, it had nothing to do with the

dinosaurs. I mean, some of my best friends are dinosaurs. Why, just yesterday I had ol' Stegosaurus and my good pal Tyrannosaurus Rex over for some chips and dip while we caught a game on the ol' tube. I tell you, that Tyrannosaurus is a real crack-up. During halftime, he talked about this new invention of his called "fire." He said he could use it to cook things and to keep himself warm at night. Yeah, right. Like, I'm going to throw out my microwave and electric blanket to try some crazy new invention of his.

Right now, though, I would have traded just about anything to get out of this predicament. I mean, you could tell by the starved look in these Brontosaurus bullies' eyes that they were wondering if I had any taste. And we aren't talkin' about whether I like Picasso or not.

"Nicholas . . . ," I said calmly, showing my courage even in the face of annihilation. "NICHOLAS!!"

But instead of coming to the rescue, my little buddy just reached his hand down and ripped off the sheet of paper to start again. I managed to jump from the old piece to the new one just before he crumpled it and tossed it into the trash. Poor Brontosaurus babies. And we were getting to be such good friends.

Still clad in my animal skins, I was now at the head of a giant ship. Only this time I was wearing a helmet with a set of horns that would turn Rudolph's nose green with envy.

Yes, it was I, Victor the Viking—obviously off to discover America.

I glanced to the left. Nothing was happening.

I glanced to the right. Nothing was happening.

I nervously cleared my throat and waited. Any minute ol' Nicky-boy would come up with some super fantasamagorical adventure in which I would be the star hero. . . .

127

Nothing.

Ahem. "Any minute now ol' Nicky-boy will come up with some super fantasmagorical . . ."

I said, "ANY MINUTE NOW OL' NICKY-BOY WILL COME UP—"

"I don't think so, McGee."

"What?"

"Not tonight," *Nicholas repeated.*

Hmmm . . . this was sounding serious. With a victorious vault that only valiant Vikings can vault, I leaped from the sketch pad and onto Nick's drawing table. "What's up, Buckaroo?"

"I don't know," *he sighed.* "It's this whole art table thing."

"Oh, that," *I said, nodding a knowing nod.*

"I have to make a decision by tomorrow, and I still don't know what to do."

"Did you make up that list?"

"Yeah."

"How'd it come out?"

"Not so good."

I waited in silence. Sometimes even valiant Vikings are at a loss for words.

"I've tried everything I know," *he said, sighing as he set his chin on the table.* "And I still don't have an answer."

"Everything?" *I asked.* "Even what your parents suggested?"

He looked up to me (which is hard to do when someone's only seven and a half inches high). "You mean . . . prayer?" *he asked.* "You think God's just going to come down out of the sky and write the answer on the wall?"

"If he did, your mom would sure get mad. She just painted it last month and—"

128

"So if he doesn't write it out for me," Nick interrupted, "how am I going to know what he wants?"

"You got me, Bub. But you'll know. Somehow, you'll know."

Nick stared at me a long moment. I could tell by the look in his eyes that he knew I had a point. Then, before I knew it, he had his head bowed. I couldn't tell what he was saying, but by the way his lips were moving I knew he was getting serious . . . real serious.

And I knew an answer would be coming.

SEVEN
Monday . . . At Last

Monday took forever to roll around. Now we all know
you're supposed to hate Mondays. It's like a law or something. Normally Sarah and Nicholas are pretty good at
obeying that law. But this Monday was an exception.
They couldn't wait for this Monday to happen.

Nicholas's reasons were simple.

Monday was the last day to make his decision about the
art table. He was so tired of going back and forth, trying to
make up his mind, that now he almost didn't care what
decision he made—just as long as he made one.

Sarah's reasons were a little different.

I mean, first there was Saturday night and the ride
home with her parents from the hospital. It was a very
silent ride. But that was OK. Sarah didn't feel much like
talking anyway.

Then there was that night's sleep. Well, OK, so *sleep*
isn't the right word. I mean, every time she managed to
close her eyes she saw that green car and her friend sailing
over the back end . . . or the blood from Bonnie's head on
her pants . . . or Jason's bored glance at her . . . or even—
even that stupid green Gummi Bear that had stuck to her
pant leg. Then, once she had seen those pictures a billion
times, they started mixing up with each other. Now she

was holding her own bleeding head, or Jason was being hit by the car (which actually looked like a huge green Gummi Bear). On and on it went like this, through the whole night.

Then came Sunday morning. Over breakfast, a very droopy-eyed Sarah finally worked up the courage to ask what her punishment would be. Unfortunately, Mom and Dad said they hadn't decided yet. Now, to anyone who's ever been a kid, that only meant one thing: It was going to be bad news. Real bad news.

Then there was Sunday school. Of course, the whole subject of the morning was—you guessed it—disobedience. If Sarah hadn't known better, she would have bet her parents had called the teacher in the middle of the night and told him what to teach on. Talk about feeling miserable. I mean, all the poor girl could do was sit and fidget and look at her watch, and sit and fidget, and then fidget some more.

Then came Sunday afternoon. And her parents' decision. We're not talking just any old decision here. We're talking the worst possible of all decisions.

Sarah had just opened up the lid to the washing machine. Try as she might, she couldn't hold back a groan. This was the second time she'd put her new white pants through the wash cycle, and it was the second time they had come out stained. She wasn't sure if it was the mud and oil from the ground, or the Gummi Bears, or the blood—or a combination of all three. But whatever it was, the stain just wouldn't come out.

"What's up?" Mom had asked as she poked her head in the doorway.

"Oh, it's these stupid pants. I can't get this spot out."

"Let me see."

There had been an uneasy silence between the two as Mom looked over the stain. Sarah had still been feeling pretty guilty about the night before. She knew she'd really let her folks down and that it might take forever to regain their trust again. If you really get down to it, that's what bothered Sarah the most: that she'd lost her folks' trust.

After another long look at the stain, Mom had begun to talk. "Your father and I have been doing a lot of thinking. You know, about your discipline for last night."

Sarah had quietly braced herself for the worst. Unfortunately, she'd had no idea how bad the worst could be.

Mom had continued. "We've decided that because of the seriousness of your disobedience . . . the lying, the deception, the blatant rebellion . . ."

Uh-oh, here it comes.

"And because you want to be treated as an adult . . ."

Sarah had slowly closed her eyes and waited.

"Well, we've decided that you're going to have to come up with your own discipline."

Sarah's eyes had popped open. *How could this be? How could she be so lucky?*

Well, at least that was what she had thought at first. . . .

But over the next few hours, it hadn't taken Sarah long to realize she wasn't as lucky as she had figured.

At first she dreamed up some drastic discipline, like having to miss all of Grandma's overcooked vegetables for the next three months. Or being forbidden from talking to her pesky little brother for a week. Or, horror of

133

horrors, having to have her own telephone installed in her bedroom.

But her folks wanted her to look at the decision like an adult. And when she started to do that—when she began to really understand the seriousness of her actions—well, suddenly, things weren't quite so easy.

Over and over again, she ran what she had done through her mind. Over and over again, she thought of what *could* have happened. And over and over again, she thought of the different punishments she should face.

Mom had given her until Monday to come up with a decision. But, like Nicholas, Sarah had grown so tired of running the choices back and forth in her mind that she almost didn't care what the punishment would be. Just as long as Monday would hurry up and come. Just as long as she could hurry up and get it over with.

Now, finally, it was here!

At precisely 8:23 A.M., Nicholas was sitting in his class-room sketching another McGee adventure as they all waited for their teacher, Mrs. Harmon, to arrive. Renee was looking over his shoulder and having a good laugh over what he was drawing.

"You know," she chuckled, "it's hard to believe you really make that stuff up."

Nick nodded. Sometimes he even surprised himself.

"So why don't you ever act as funny as McGee?" she asked.

Suddenly he stopped nodding. Now he wasn't sure if that was a compliment or not. But, whatever it was, it started him thinking.

Uh-oh, it's decision time again. Let's take a look and see what's going through the little guy's mind this time.

QUESTION: WOULD I BE MORE POPULAR IF I ACTED LIKE McGEE?

Hmmm . . . Well, my answer is a definite yes! But, for the sake of science and considering all the angles, let's just press these buttons here, load in the Imagination Program, and . . . All right, who let their Gooey-Nut Bar melt all over the Synaptic Crystals? How do you expect anybody to make clear decisions when his mind's full of all this sugary garbage? This sticky, gooey, yummy, scrumptious, knock-your-socks-off, incredible-tasting garbage?

Well, I suppose somebody has to clean up this mess. So . . .

SLURRRRRRP.

Burp!

Ahhhhh . . . much better. Now, where were we? Oh yes, the Imagination Program. Let's drop it in and take a look.

Check it out—there's Mrs. Harmon coming into the classroom. Let me turn up the volume a little.

"All right, class. Who would like to give their book report first?"

Now she's looking over the kids. Wait a minute! Something's wrong. She looks like she's seen a ghost. No, it's not a ghost, it's . . . it's . . .

"Nicholas?" *she asks, looking slightly stunned.*

Sure 'nuff, it's Nicholas. Only now he's the best-looking Nicholas you've ever seen. From his red high-tops and yellow/orange suspenders, to his blond hair combed up just like mine, he looks like . . . like . . . Hey, ya know what? He looks like me! No wonder he's so handsome, so dashing, so

135

incredibly well dressed, and . . . did I mention handsome?
Well, well, well—the kid's trying to be me!

Now he's leaping to his feet.

"That's my name," he's answering Mrs. Harmon, "don't
wear it out—yuk, yuk, yuk." Not exactly a great imitation of
my incredible comic genius, but, hey, at least the kid's trying.

It must not be too bad a try, 'cause the rest of the class is just
sitting there, staring in amazement.

"So what d'ya say, Teach," he's asking. "Can I get started
on the old review-a-roo?"

Mrs. Harmon seems to be speechless, too. In fact, it's all she
can do just to nod her head.

OK, let's fast-forward this a little and see what happens.
BREE-LEEEEEEEEEEEE . . .

Ah, here's the class again. Hmmm, their mouths are still
hanging open. There's Nick in front of them. Hold it a minute.
Not only is he giving his book report, it looks like he's playing
one of the characters—complete with plastic sword and eye
patch!

"Harr, Matey . . . shiver me timbers. Batten down me
hatches, hoist the mainsail, and all those other kinda
salty sayings. If ya don't tell me where ye've hidden me
treasure, I'll have yur head, or my name ain't Long John
Underwear, er, Long John Silver. Har-har-har."

Hold the phone! Look at those kids' faces! That's not amazement—that's distaste, that's disgust, and . . . oh no, could it
be? Say it isn't so! But yes, yes, it's the worst of all possible
things! That actually looks like boredom on their faces!

Can you believe it? Me, boring?? Me, the incredible,
one-and-only McGee? I know it's only Nick trying to imitate
me, but still . . . an imitation of me is better than no me.

136

Then again, maybe that's the problem. Maybe there's only room for one "one-and-only" me. Sure, it's great my little buddy wants to be like me. (And why not? How could you ask for a better role model?) But still . . . maybe he should just try staying himself.

"To McGee or not to McGee," that is the question. Well, by the expression on the kids' faces it looks like they already have the answer. So does Mrs. Harmon. Even Nicholas is starting to get the point. What's that he's saying?

"Come on guys, these are jokes . . . they're supposed to be funny."

No sale. The kids aren't buying it. In fact, they look more boringly bored than before.

"What are you guys? An oil painting?"

Hmmm, I see their point. That may be one of my favorite lines, but even I can see how Nick is kind of . . . I hate to admit it . . . obnoxious. I mean, let's face it, this thing just ain't flying. Nick's definitely caught on to the fact, too. Look at that, he's even starting to sweat a little. Yes-siree-bob, I'd say our boy blunder's had enough, wouldn't you? (I know I have.) So let's go ahead and punch the Decision button.

CONCLUSION: DON'T BE SOMEONE ELSE. . . . BE YOURSELF!

I'll eat to that. Now where'd that Gooey-Nut Bar go?

EIGHT
3:37 P.M.

On the way home from school, Sarah thought she'd
swing by Bonnie's to see how she was. Bonnie had been
released from the hospital Sunday afternoon. But she
hadn't made it to school today. From what Sarah saw as
she entered her friend's bedroom, it looked like she
wouldn't be making it to school for quite a few days.

"Hi," Sarah said as she came in.

Bonnie turned from the trillionth rerun of *Gilligan's
Island*.

"Hi, yourself," she mumbled.

Sarah barely heard. She barely noticed Bonnie had
spoken. What she did notice was how bad Bonnie
looked. I mean, it was more than the huge bandage over
her forehead or the cast on her leg or the throbbing head-
ache she kept complaining about. It was even more than
the bedpan she had to keep nearby to throw up in . . .
something she'd been doing a lot of.

The fact is, Bonnie looked just plain bad. No question
about it. I mean, if you didn't know any better, you
would have thought she'd been hit by a car or something.
Which makes sense, since she had.

Sarah tried to put on her best smile. You know, the

139

type where you're trying so hard to look happy that you're not even sure what the other person is saying?

It took a little doing, but Sarah finally was able to cheer Bonnie up a little. Maybe it had something to do with them getting down to the important information. You know, like who is mad at whom, who's going with whom, and, of course, who Mr. Seneca—the awesomely handsome and incredibly single English teacher—is currently dating. You know, important stuff like that.

But during the whole conversation, one thought kept haunting Sarah. She just couldn't shake it. No matter what she said or how she said it, the thought just kept coming back to her: *This could be you lying in this bed.*

It was nearly an hour before their conversation died down. Bonnie was getting tired and needed some rest. At last, Sarah was able to leave. Of course, she promised to swing by again. And, of course, she'd be happy to drop off Bonnie's homework. But when Sarah finally stepped outside, it was like a breath of fresh air—like she could finally breathe again.

Yes, that could have been her in that bed. OK, so her parents set up some rough rules. Sometimes they seemed impossibly strict. But they had their reasons . . . like making sure she didn't end up like Bonnie.

Sarah sighed. So the rules had a reason for being there. Now all she had to do was think up the right punishment for not following them. . . .

"Hey, what's the big rush?" Louis asked as he and Nick left the school and raced for the bike racks.

"I'm going over to Graham's art store," Nicholas answered.

"So, you gonna make up your mind about the art table?"

"Yeah," Nick sighed as he started dialing the combination on his lock, "one way or the other. You want to come along?"

"Oh, yeah." Louis grinned as he popped the lock off his own bike. "Sounds like nonstop action to me."

Nick grinned back. He knew that deciding on a new art table didn't rate real high on Louis's Things-I-Just-Have-to-Do-before-I-Die list. But he also knew Louis was a friend. And because it was important to Nick, it would be important to Louis. "Race you!" he shouted as he pushed off on his bike.

"You're on!" Louis shouted back as he hopped on his bike and followed.

Meanwhile, Sarah was up in her room when she heard a gentle knock on her door. *Uh-oh*, she thought. *Here it comes.*

"Sweetheart . . ." It was Dad. "Can you come on downstairs a minute? Your mother and I want to talk to you."

"OK, Dad," Sarah answered. She tried to sound as cheery as possible . . . considering she was heading for her own execution.

The trip down the stairs seemed to take forever. When she rounded the corner, it was just as she expected. There were her parents sitting in the family room, waiting. Mom was folding laundry. Dad had been reading the paper.

"Well," she sighed under her breath, "here goes nothing."

141

At first they talked a little bit about school. Then a little bit about Bonnie. Finally they got to the real reason for the little pow-wow.

"So . . . ," Dad asked, "have you reached a decision about your discipline?"

"I think so." Sarah nodded. Her voice croaked just a little. It was funny, but she almost sounded like Nick when he was nervous. She looked at her parents. They waited in silence. Then, taking a deep breath, she began.

"What I did was wrong. I mean, everything about it was wrong. I lied about going to Bonnie's, I disobeyed about going to the races. I mean, everything. It was . . . it was just all wrong."

She glanced up at her parents.

They waited in silence.

"And . . ." She swallowed, then continued. "Well, I think maybe grounding me for," she hesitated a second. This was going to be harder than she'd thought. "Grounding me until Christmas vacation, well, I think that would teach me my lesson."

Mom and Dad exchanged glances. More silence. Finally Dad spoke. He looked a little concerned. "Honey . . . Christmas vacation is more than two months away."

Sarah could feel her eyes starting to burn. Any moment the tears would spill onto her cheeks. "Daddy, I know it should be longer, but I really wanted to go to the basketball tournament this year. Maybe, maybe after the tournament we could go back to grounding me, you know, until . . ."

"No, sweetheart, that's not what we meant," her mom

142

quietly interrupted. For a second Sarah thought she saw just a trace of a smile.

"You've obviously thought this over pretty carefully," Dad said.

"Yes, sir."

"You've thought about all of the rules you broke and all of the reasons we made those rules."

"Yes, sir," she repeated.

"Well," he said, glancing toward Mom for agreement. "I think two and a half months is a little tougher than what we had in mind."

At first Sarah couldn't believe her ears.

"You see, sweetheart," her mom joined in, "we don't punish you to make you suffer. We just want to give you a discipline strong enough that you'll remember . . . to teach you so you'll learn."

Dad continued, "The very fact that you took so long to think over your discipline . . . well, that by itself must have been a pretty strong lesson."

"One of the toughest," Sarah agreed with a long sigh.

Mom and Dad exchanged smiles.

"That's what we were hoping for," Mom admitted.

Sarah's heart was starting to race. This was getting too good to be true. It was like some fairy tale with an and-they-lived-happily-ever-after ending. "So you mean," she asked excitedly, "that my making the decision was enough? Now I'm off the hook! No punish—"

"Not quite, young lady," Dad interrupted.

Sarah frowned slightly. Well, so much for fairy-tale endings.

143

"I think, though, that being grounded for four weeks should be enough," Dad finished.

"And no telephone privileges," Mom threw in.

Sarah's heart sank a little, but not much. I mean, let's face it, four weeks was a far cry from two and a half months.

"Thanks, guys," she exclaimed. And before she knew it, she was once again in their arms. First Mom's, then Dad's.

"Listen," Mom said. "Old moneybags here," she gave a poke at Dad, "promised to take us out to dinner when Nick gets home from the art store. Why don't you go change clothes?"

"Into what?" Sarah frowned. For a moment the dark cloud of gloom she'd been walking under for the past couple of days returned. "I spent all my money on those white pants, and now I don't have anything to wear."

"Not quite." Mom smiled. She reached over to the pile of laundry she'd been folding and produced the pants. "Why don't you try these?"

Sarah couldn't believe her eyes as Mom handed the white pants to her. "Look at this!" she cried as she turned the pants over and over in her hands. "The stain's completely gone! How'd you do it?"

"Experience," Mom said, grinning.

"They're perfect!" Sarah held them against her. They looked great—as clean and new as when she first bought them. "Thanks, Mom!" She gave her mom another hug and whirled around toward the stairs.

"Though your sins are as scarlet," Dad quoted softly, "they'll be white as snow."

"What's that, dear?" Mom asked.

But before Dad could answer—in fact, before Sarah had even reached the stairs—Nick suddenly barged into the room.

"Well, kiddo," Dad asked. "What's the verdict? Did you get it?"

"Get what?" Nick asked.

For a moment everyone came to a stop. They looked at each other. Then in perfect unison they shouted, "The new drawing table!" (Though Sarah was the only one that added the phrase *idiot child* at the end.)

"Oh, that." Nick couldn't help but break into a grin. "Not exactly," he answered. And with that he reached into his backpack and pulled out a new tablet. "I decided to buy a sketch pad instead."

"But why?" Sarah asked in astonishment. "I mean, all week you've been talking—"

"I know, I know," he interrupted. "I just . . . I guess I just realized that a table like that was . . . well, I'm not really ready for something so fancy."

Everyone stood in silence as he continued.

"I got to thinking about all the time it took me to make that money, and the other things I could do with it—like buy a bike or help other people and stuff."

Mom and Dad were more than a little surprised . . . not to mention pleased. Come to think of it, so was Sarah. Being the older sister, it was her job to look for opportunities to use little brothers to little advantages. And right now, she thought she spotted one of those ways.

"You know, Nicky, old friend," she said as she lovingly put her arm around him.

Nick glanced at his parents. *"Nicky, old friend"*? What

was this all about? They were supposed to be brother and sister. That meant nonstop war two weeks past forever. What was this "Nicky, old friend" stuff?

It didn't take long to find out.

"Maybe," Sarah continued, "just maybe you and I should go in together to buy a car. . . ."

"A car?" Nick's voice cracked.

"Sure! What better way to spend that money?" She was guiding him toward the stairs. "I mean, I get my permit next year and everything. Now of course you wouldn't be old enough to drive right away, but I'd take care of it for you, and you could ride in it sometimes, and—"

"Sometimes?" Nick protested.

"Well, it's only fair. I mean, I don't want to chauffeur some little kid all around—"

"Who are you calling a kid?"

"Well, you're certainly not Mr. Maturity. I mean, look at that shirt, those pants."

"What's wrong with these . . . ?"

The rest of the argument was lost as the two headed up the stairs.

Mom and Dad glanced over to each other.

Things were finally getting back to normal.

NINE
Wrapping Up

Thus ends another fun-filled, all-expense-paid journey (except for the bucks you laid out for this book) into the life and times of one Nicholas Martin, K.E. (Kid Extraordinaire).

Hey, it's been a kick. A real slice. I'll tell you one thing, I've decided decisions are tough customers. Sure, sure, no one said they'd be easy. And the older we get, the more we'll probably have to make 'em. So I guess it doesn't hurt to start practicing now. . . . Right?

I did spot one trick I plan to use, though. It was Nick's three-step plan: Listen to advice, make out a list, and check out what the Boss (better known as "God") has in mind. I figure the last one's the most important. I mean, when you think about it, I suppose God's been around a couple of years more than most of us. So it's no wonder he has some pretty good ideas about things.

Anyway, I'm glad that's over with for now. At least until the next time. And, hey, thanks for stopping by the ol' Brain Screen Room. Now, watch your head as you go out, and be sure to shut the door behind you. It's pretty chilly out there, and, as you know, I like to keep Nick full of as much hot air as possible.

So, to all you kids and kidettes . . . ta-ta, au revoir,

*arrivederci, and all that fancy "catch ya later" sort of stuff.
We'll see you again for our next exciting, action-packed
adventure—same McGee time, same McGee station. Hmmm,
speaking of stations, I wonder if I can pick up* World Cham-
pionship Wrestling *on this screen? . . . Maybe if I disconnect
this red wire and twist it onto this green one—*

ZZZZTT!!

Groan . . . *anybody got some aspirin?*

'Twas the Fight before Christmas

by Bill Myers

Don't look to men for help; their greatest leaders fail. . . . But happy is the man who has the God of Jacob as his helper, whose hope is in the Lord his God. (Psalm 146:3, 5, *The Living Bible*)

ONE
Major Mishap to the Rescue!

*It was a dark and stormy night. Wind blew. Rain poured.
Waves crashed. (I'd say that about covers it for dark and
stormy nights, wouldn't you?) Everywhere water cascaded upon
the shipwrecked survivors. It looked hopeless for them as they
desperately clung to the side of their life raft—a life raft that
looked suspiciously like a giant soap dish. Suddenly, cutting
through the waves, appeared the good and mighty ship S.S.
Rubber Ducky!*

*A cheer sprang from the survivors. They were saved! They
would live. Once again they would be free to ponder life's most
puzzling questions. Once again they would be free to ask why
they had to learn the multiplication tables when everyone and
his brother owns a pocket calculator. And once again—*

*But wait! Suddenly from the dark, murky depths swam up
the fierce and treacherous sea monster known throughout the
world simply as "Wash Cloth." Before Ducky knew what hit
him, Cloth surrounded him from underneath, covered him
with his thick, nappy hide, and began dragging him to the
bottom of the ocean.*

"Quack, quack, choke, choke, glug, glug . . ."

*The survivors watched in horror as their last hope disap-
peared into the—*

151

RING . . .

As their last and final hope disappeared into the—

RING . . .

It was the phone. Rats. I hate it when that happens. Nothing destroys a good bathtub fantasy like a telephone call.

RING . . .

All right, already. Hold on to your sea horses.

"Hello," *I said.* "Clark Cant here."

"Clark?"

I immediately recognized the voice on the other end. It belonged to our beloved leader, the president. "Clark," *he repeated,* "do you have a mirror in your room?"

What a stupid question. With my incredible good looks and appreciation of beauty, how could I not have a mirror in the room? Actually in every room. Actually dozens in every room.

I threw a look over to my gorgeous reflection and let out a gasp. Where was my tan? What had happened to my gorgeously bronzed body? All those hours at the tanning salon and for what? All I had to show for it was a body that looked . . . how could it be? . . . but my skin . . . it looked gray! I glanced up to my beautiful baby blues. Double gasp! They were also gray! And my lovely blond locks. Gasp! Gasp! Gasp! Everywhere I looked, everything I saw—it was awful, but everything was a terrible, boring shade of (you guessed it) gray.

"Clark," *the president continued,* "you need to contact Major Mishap for us. His archrival, the fiendish French freak, Monsieur Mon O. Chrome, is on the loose again. He has stolen all of the world's colors and is holding them hostage inside his giant blimp."

Quicker than you can say "Is it just my imagination or are these McGee tales getting weirder?" I hopped into my Mishap Mobile and raced off. I was looking for the nearest tollbooth in which to change. (I prefer a phone booth, but some other superhero owns the franchise on those, so I go for the next best thing.) Finding an empty tollbooth, I leaped out of my car and was immediately transformed from the mild-mannered Clark Cant into the world-famous crime fighter and acne-free good guy, Major Mishap!

With my cape flapping heroically in the wind, I took a mighty leap and flew into the air. I sailed magnificently—for about three feet before doing a dynamic nosedive into the concrete. My ever-so-keen intellect told me something wasn't quite right. Immediately I checked the batteries in my cape. Hmmm, just as I suspected. My A.C. had gone D.C. through the polarization of my whatchamacallits. (Translation: The only way I was going to get airborne was to find a good plane.)

Fortunately, a Hertz Rent-a-Jet just happened to be landing nearby, so I quickly filled out the forms, left the birthright to my firstborn as deposit, pulled back the throttle, and roared into the wild gray yonder.

From high in the sky, things looked worse than I had expected. Without color, everything was an awful shade of drab. I mean, it was as boring as your grandmother's old photo album. No color anywhere—just black, white, and gray. It was worse than the first part of The Wizard of Oz, before Dorothy lands in Munchkinville.

And then I saw it. . . .

High overhead was Mon O. Chrome's blimp—its sides bulging from all the colors it was holding prisoner.

My radio crackled to life. "So you've finally found me?"

It was Mon O. Chrome. There was no mistaking it. His

voice was as boring as everything else about him. Poor guy. Even his autobiography, My Greatest Most Super-Keen Adventures of All Times, *was a bore. In fact, it was so boring that doctors around the world prescribed it to patients who couldn't sleep. "Just read two of these paragraphs, and call me in the morning," they'd say.*

And it always worked!

So now, Monsieur Mon O. was set on making the rest of the world as boring as he was.

"Mon O.," I called through the radio, "You haven't got a chance. Give up while there's still time."

But instead of an answer he began growling and barking. That's right . . . growling and barking.

Well, you didn't have to be a rocket scientist to figure out what that meant. The man obviously wanted (here it comes) a "dog fight." (Look, I warned you.) That was fine with me. If he wanted to battle it out in the skies, we'd battle it out in the skies.

But before I had a chance to form one of my fabulous plans, he threw his blimp into hyperboogie and came at me with his guns a-blazing.

Fortunately, because of my incredible flying skills (not to mention my dashing good looks), I was able to outmaneuver him. In fact, my skills were so great that as I zoomed past him I could see the poor guy already turning gray with envy.

"Mon O.," I tried to reason, "give it up. This is your last warning."

No answer. Instead he pulled up, shot high over my head, opened up his bomb bay doors, and began dropping water balloons. Only instead of water, they were filled with paint. Awful drab colors of gray and black.

154

Ker-splash, ker-splosh, KER-SPLAT!

It was the "ker-splat" that got me. And it got me good. Right across the ol' windshield. I was blinded. I couldn't see a thing. Before I knew it, my plane dipped into a steep dive and began falling, out of control. I fought to pull it back up. But since I had no idea where up was, I wasn't as successful as I could have been.

"NICHOLAS!" I shouted.

It's not like I was scared or anything. But we cartoon characters always call out to our creators when we're about to be destroyed, pulverized, and/or smashed to bits. I think it's a law or something. And, always being one to obey the law . . .

"N I C H O L A S ! ! !"

But Nicholas was nowhere to be found. I had no alternative. Without a word I did the most heroic thing possible. I bailed. Before you could say "Hey, it's been real, I've had a great time, but now I gotta go," I reached down and pressed the ol' Eject button.

K-SWOOOOOOOOSHHHHHHH!

I shot out of that cockpit faster than kids out of a classroom the last day of school. Higher and higher I flew. Right past the blimp and the laughing Monsieur Mon O.

I pulled my ripcord and watched as my parachute opened up. Gently I began floating back down. Now, normally the game would have been up. Normally ol' Mon O. boy would have won. But since I'm supposed to be the superhero in this story, and since my name's on the cover of this book . . . well, what other choice did I have? I'm supposed to win, right? It's in my contract.

So, of course, a brilliant thought flashed through my mind. I reached into my backpack and pulled out my steel-cleated golf

155

shoes—the very shoes I carry for just such occasions. Quickly, I slipped them on.

The blimp was right below me. I carefully maneuvered my parachute until my steel cleats landed right smack dab in the center of the overstuffed balloon. And, sure enough . . .

K-BLAM!

I ripped a hole in that puppy the size of Pinocchio's nose on a good day of lying. Before ol' Mon O. knew what had hit him, he was zipping back and forth across the sky, completely out of control.

SWIIISH! SWOOOSH! SWAAASH!

Colors were spurting out of my custom-designed opening and going in all directions. It was a sight to behold as the colors fell back to earth, replacing all those ugly blacks and grays with their true hues. Once again the Golden Gate Bridge turned golden. Once again the blue skies of Montana turned blue. And once again Detroit turned . . . well, Detroit's always been gray. But, hey, two out of three ain't bad.

Yes-siree-bob. Another dramatic drama dramatically done by the one and only—tum-da-da—Major Mishap.

Now if I can just get back to my bath and Yellow Ducky before the bubbles are all gone. . . .

TWO
The Tragic Pageant

While McGee was inside Nicholas's sketch pad enjoying his fantasy as Major Mishap, Nicholas was undergoing his own fantasy. Well, really it was more of a nightmare than a fantasy. At the moment, he was rehearsing for the annual Eastfield Elementary School Christmas Pageant. No problem there. Nick loved being in the pageant. The problem lay in the fact that there were only three days left before the show. The cast and crew needed a little more time than three days. Actually, they needed a lot more time than three days. Actually, the way this pageant was going, they could have used three years.

In short, the show was awful!

First, there was the Santa Claus—played by Philip. Nice guy, Philip. Ever since Nicholas had offered to skateboard against Derrick Cryder on Philip's behalf, they had been good friends. No doubt about it, Philip was a good kid. The only problem was this kid didn't know beans about acting. So instead of his Santa Claus giving a mighty "Ho-Ho-Ho!" Philip's version came out sounding a little more like "Squeak-Squeak-Squeak."

Now, to be fair, Philip's acting wasn't the main problem. The fact is, his squeaks had more to do with his size than his talent. I mean, this guy was so small he looked like he had to hop out of the bathtub before draining it just so he wouldn't get sucked under. But everyone figured with enough stuffing and pillows, he'd make an OK Santa. Unfortunately, the weight of all that stuffing and those pillows kept toppling him over . . . usually right onto his face. Poor guy. It was all he could do just to keep his balance, let alone deliver his lines.

So, instead of a Jolly Old Elf, this Santa looked like a Tipsy Old Munchkin as he stumbled, staggered, and squeaked.

Not a pleasant sight.

Even so, it wasn't as bad as the dancing snowflakes. Again, it probably wasn't their fault that the record they were practicing to kept skipping. It wasn't their fault that it kept repeating the same three notes over and over again. It wasn't their fault that in trying to keep up with it, they were dancing themselves into a frenzied state of oblivion.

Normally, Mrs. Harmon would have been there to unstick the needle, but at the moment she was trying to reason with someone playing a shepherdess. The girl kept insisting that her little kitten needed to be in the show, that she would make a great lamb . . .

"Oh, pleeease, Mrs. Harmon. This could be Fluffy's big break. She loves show business, and she won't be any trouble."

Mrs. Harmon threw a doubtful glance at Brutus—a giant St. Bernard, who was already having a major barking attack, all because of little Fluffy. Brutus's master was trying to stick some cardboard antlers on his head so he would pass as a reindeer. But old Brutus wasn't interested in being a reindeer. He was interested in being a dog—a dog that barks at, chases, and maybe even eats cats.

Somewhere amidst all this craziness, our young hero, Nicholas Martin, stood buried under a bathrobe seven sizes too big and a giant oversized turban that kept falling down over his face. Nicholas, Louis, and Derrick had been chosen to play the three wise men. No problem there. Of course, wise men need to wear beards. Still no problem. The problem was that only two out of the three wise men's beards were sticking to their faces. And since Nick was never the luckiest of persons, well, you can imagine whose beard was not staying up.

"It's not going to stick," he kept complaining to his older sister, Sarah.

But big sister Sarah, who was chomping away on about twelve sticks of Juicy Fruit, would not take no for an answer. She was almost fifteen. She knew how to handle these types of things. She knew how to handle everything.

At the other end of the stage, Mrs. Harmon finally managed to reach the record player. With an awful *zipppppppp* she lifted the needle, scraping it across every groove of the record.

Everyone groaned and cringed.

But Mrs. Harmon paid no attention. "All right," she called, clapping her hands. "I need all the snowflakes over here, please. All the snowflakes."

By now the snowflakes were so dizzy from dancing to the skipping record that they could barely stay on their feet as they staggered toward her.

159

Meanwhile, Derrick couldn't resist the temptation to throw a jab in Nicholas's direction. "Hear that, Martin. She wants all the 'flakes' over there."

Nick turned to fire off a nifty comeback, but his head was suddenly yanked around by Sarah. "Will you hold still!" she ordered as she continued to work on the beard. By now she was snapping her gum like there was no tomorrow.

Not far away Renee—good ol' fashion-conscious, every-hair-in-place Renee—was going through her own struggle. She'd been chosen to play the donkey. Not her idea of a great role, but she went along with it. She even agreed to get in the bottom half of the costume, the part with the tail and hoofs and everything. Of course, that didn't mean she wouldn't complain. I mean, after all, she was Renee.

"Look at the waistline on this thing," she whined. "I've heard of the baggy look, but this is ridiculous!"

Now if that had been her only problem, Renee probably would have survived. But it was the giant papier-mâché donkey head coming her way that really ruined her day. "Hold it," she protested. "No way am I wearing that. I just spent $79.95 on a perm, and I'm not going to hide it under some—"

But she was too late. Before she could finish her sentence, Louis's mom had plopped it on top of her head.

After a moment, Renee cleared her throat. "You sure Tina Turner started out this way?" she said, her voice echoing inside the hollow head.

"Trust me," Louis's mom answered.

Meanwhile, our little Santa was walking toward Mrs. Harmon. Well, walking may not be the right word. It was more like stumbling and falling, and stumbling and falling, and stumbling and falling. He was making pretty good progress, though. That is, until he finally arrived . . . and realized he couldn't stop.

Before he could warn the unsuspecting snowflakes . . .

OOAAFF! BUMP! BANG! He crashed head-on into the first flake, and snowflake number one, still tipsy from her dance with the skipping record, fell face first into snowflake number two, who toppled into snowflake number three, who . . . well, I think you get the picture. It was like a giant row of dominoes as all six snowflakes fell into each other and tumbled down to the floor.

It was a sight to behold. A work of art. That is, until Brutus leaped into the pile and began licking every face he could get his wet, slobbery, tongue on.

"Ick! *Cough! Gag!"* the girls cried.

"*Bark! Bark! Bark!"* Brutus replied.

"Heel, Brutus, heel!" the owner cried.

But no matter how hard the owner pulled or how hard the snowflakes pushed, Brutus just kept coming in for more licks. To him it was a fun, free-for-all game of Pig Pile. To the girls it was a fight for their lives as they kicked and squirmed to avoid the attack of the slurping tongue.

The rest of the cast crowded around for a better look. Soon everyone was having a good laugh. Well, almost everyone. It's not that Mrs. Harmon wasn't having fun. But somewhere underneath that smile there was the look of panic. She knew they had only three days left . . . and she was beginning to hope she could find a less stressful job—maybe as an air traffic controller.

Things were looking brighter for Sarah. In a flash of inspiration she had the solution to Nick's problem. As his beard fell from his chin for the zillionth time, Sarah suddenly spit out her gum, plopped it on the furry hair piece, and quickly stuck it to his chin. Bingo! A perfect solution!

Well, almost perfect. The sick look on Nick's face said it wasn't quite what he'd had in mind. But before he had a chance to complain, McGee suddenly showed up. . . .

Yes-siree-bob, leave it to my intense intellectual intelligence to figure that Nicky boy and the gang needed a little help. And since "Help" is my middle name—along, of course, with "Humble," "Heroic," "Handsome," and . . . (did I say "Humble?"), well, I had no choice but to save the day. Now, to say that their show was a complete disaster probably isn't fair. It would be fair to say that if they were really lucky, the world might come to an end before opening night.

So without speaking another word, a tremendous sacrifice on my part, I leaped from Nick's notebook and began doing my voice exercises.

"Why voice exercises?" you're asking. Well, my dear reader, that's elementary. As the world's greatest actor with the world's greatest voice, I have to take care of that voice by warming it up. Particularly if I am going to give another one of my world-famous, show-stopping performances.

Yes, it was I, the Magnificent McGee—watched and admired by millions . . . well, all right, watched and admired by thousands . . . hundreds? . . . OK, so Mom and Dad

thought I wasn't half bad and agreed to watch me on Sunday
afternoons if I paid them a buck fifty apiece and if there was
nothing on TV.

Anyway, I grabbed my spray bottle, hopped onto a nearby
ladder, and began warming up with my favorite voice exercise.
I'm not sure why it's my favorite. Maybe it has something to do
with the lyrics. . . .

"Me-me-me-me-me-me-me."

Oh, how I love those words.

"Me-me-me-me-me-me-me."

Such meaning, such depth. . . .

"Me-me-me—"

Just then the phone rang. No doubt it was the famous film
director, Steven Spellbound. Either him or his good buddy
George Mucus. Poor guys. No matter how many times I tell
them I'm not interested in starring in their next flicks, they just
keep on asking.

I picked up the phone and answered, "Hey, babe, sweet-
heart, buddy boy, love ya, you're magic, don't ever change, let's
do lunch." (That's Hollywoodese for "Hello.")

It wasn't Steven. Or even George. Instead, it was William
Shakesfear. He wanted me to star in some newfangled play
of his called Macbeth. I told him if he changed the spelling
of the last half of the title from "Beth" to "Gee," we
might have a deal. But only after I saved my little buddy's
show.

With that, I grabbed my favorite pair of solar-powered angel
wings, slipped them on, and began practicing my part. With
a hefty clearing of my throat and in my wonderful tenor voice,
I began: "McGee . . . or not McGee. That is the question."

Almost immediately Nick spotted me and asked in his

kindest, most sympathetic voice, "McGee, what do you think you're doing?"

(That's what I like about Nicholas. He's never one to let his sentimentality get out of hand.)

"Why, I'm practicing my part," I explained.

"Part?" he asked. "Your part as who?"

"Why, as Hark," I answered.

"Hark?" he challenged.

"Yeah, you know . . . 'Hark, the Herald Angel'?

But before Nick could fall down laughing over my wonderful wit, somebody suddenly grabbed the ladder I was standing on and started to walk off.

"Woooaaaaahhhhhhh!" I shouted as I lost my balance and started to fall.

Nick cringed and waited for the crash. But nothing happened. Instead, when he finally opened his eyes, he saw me giving those solar-powered angel wings a pretty good workout. What can I say? The fact of the matter is that I am a great flyer. First I flew past him right side up. Then upside down. Next I tried the Australian crawl, then finally the ever-popular backstroke.

"A piece of cake," I bragged as I fluttered effortlessly to the ground. "Pretty impressive, huh?"

But before Nicholas could voice his overwhelming admiration, some stagehand's size thirteen construction boot crashed down on top of me, flattening me flatter than a flannelgraph flapjack.

Nicholas tried his best to ease my pain with a little humor. "Yeah, McGee, I guess you could say you were a real smash."

"Mo, Mo," I mumbled through my flattened mouth. "Mery munny . . . mery munny."

164

Before Nicholas could show me any more of his under-whelming sympathy and concern, the giant turban on his head fell completely over his face.

"That's great, Squid," a sarcastic voice commented. I looked around to find the source of the sarcasm. It was Derrick Cryder, the all-American bad egg. He and Louis were walking toward us. "The more of your face you cover with that turban," Cryder continued, "the better you look."

Now it's true, Derrick was never the happiest of hoods . . . unless of course he happened to be beating somebody up. But today he seemed even more unhappy than usual.

"Hey, Derrick," Louis countered. "Why aren't you wearing your hat thing?"

"Get outta here! You morons think I'm actually gonna do this junk!" Derrick had such a gentle way with words. "You two clowns will be the only guys standing here Christmas Eve when the curtain goes up."

Unfortunately, Derrick didn't see Mrs. Harmon approaching. Even more unfortunately, her nerves were so fried she was even grouchier than Derrick. "The script calls for three wise men," she growled. "And come Friday, Mr. Cryder, three wise men is what we'll have."

Derrick spun around, a snappy comeback ready to fly. But Mrs. H. wasn't finished.

"Unless, of course, you want to be the first person in the history of Eastfield to take my class three years in a row."

Derrick was speechless. Mrs. Harmon was a teacher. A role model. She was supposed to play fair. But this . . . "This . . . this is blackmail!" he finally sputtered.

"That's right," she said as she headed backstage, grinning like she was suddenly feeling better. "Merry Christmas."

165

Derrick just stood there staring.

The kids chuckled.

Derrick glared.

And I coughed. Actually, I coughed a lot of
coughs—*anything to get ol' Nicky boy's attention so he could*
start scraping me off the floor.

166

THREE
The Gift of the Magi

By the time rehearsal was over, it was already getting dark outside. That was one of the nice things about Christmastime in Eastfield. Each day the sun seemed to set just a little earlier. And with each setting sun, peace and calm seemed to creep over the city. People buttoned up their coats just a little tighter, parents inched up their car heaters just a little warmer, children snuggled up to fireplaces and heating grates just a little closer. In short, each day as Christmas approached, everything became just a little bit cozier.

Nicholas loved this time of day—right after sunset but just before night. It was a magical time. A time when there was no sun but still plenty of light. A time of stillness, when everyone's work for the day was over. A time when a person could really slow down and think about stuff.

On this particular day there was something that made the time even more special. . . .

It was snowing.

It had started late that morning and continued all through the afternoon. It wasn't a heavy snow. It was in no hurry to throw its weight around and try to change the world. Instead, it was a gentle snow. A quiet snow.

167

A snow that came down slow and easy, softening the hard corners of the city, blurring the sharp edges of wire fences and rusty fire escapes until they were buried under a sparkling blanket. A snow that slowly covered the dirt and grime of streets and turned them into mystical paths of whiteness.

It was as if the weather knew Jesus' birthday was coming—and that his birthday was the chance for the world once again to be made clean and fresh and pure.

Nicholas felt all these things, but somehow he couldn't put them into words . . . not yet. Maybe later when he became a painter or writer or poet or something. But for right now all he knew was that the falling snow, the fading light, and the twinkling Christmas decorations in the store windows were all so perfect that it practically made his chest ache with pleasure.

And he expressed that pleasure the way any red-blooded kid would express it: He shuffled through the snow, slid across icy spots on sidewalks, and fired off the obligatory snowballs at Louis. Normally the two wouldn't be this far downtown, but Nicholas had something very special he wanted to show his buddy.

At first the gift shop didn't look like much—just a little hole in the wall whose window was filled with the usual Christmas stuff. But once the bell jingled and the boys stepped inside . . . well, it was like a miniature wonderland overflowing with old-fashioned Christmas gifts. Wooden rocking horses, gingham dolls, a thousand burning candles all giving off different scents, antique tree ornaments, wooden flutes, nutcracker soldiers as big as men or as tiny as thimbles, electric trains that chugged and whistled all over the shop . . . and the list went on and on and on.

But none of that interested Nicholas. What really interested him was the glass display case directly in front of where he and Louis stood. Without a word Nick stooped down to the lowest shelf. Louis joined him.

There, right in front of them, was the most beautiful music box they had ever seen. Its beauty wasn't in fancy silver, gold inlays, or glittery pearl ornaments. Its beauty lay in its gentle, hand-carved simplicity.

A kindly old shopkeeper approached the boys from behind the counter. Nicholas looked up to her and gave a smile. She returned it generously, catching a glint of candlelight in her eyes. Nick and the old lady had slowly become good friends. Each day for nearly two weeks Nick had swung by the shop to check on the music box. And each day for two weeks the box had lain there unpurchased. In just a couple more days Nicholas would save up enough allowance to finally buy it. And in just a couple more days his mom would have the best Christmas gift she had ever received.

Without a word, the old lady carefully lifted the box from the display case and delicately set it on the counter. The boys rose to their feet and continued to stare.

It was magnificent.

Nicholas reached out and gently opened its lid. It softly began to chime a beautiful and haunting melody—"Carol of the Bells."

"That's Mom's favorite Christmas carol," Nick whispered.

Louis nodded in silent awe. He could understand why.

Time seemed to stand still as all three faces, bathed in flickering candlelight, watched and listened.

Suddenly there was a loud *CRASH!* Nicholas and Louis spun around to see three larger boys hop over a broken oil lamp and race toward the door. The oldest-looking boy was stuffing something inside his leather coat.

"You there! Stop! Stop, I say!" It was the shopkeeper's husband. He had spotted them from the back and began chasing after them. But his age was no match for their youth.

Then Nicholas saw something that took his breath away. One of the three boys, the smallest, was Derrick Cryder!

"Stop! Thieves!" The old man continued the chase as each of the boys jostled past Nicholas and Louis on their way out the door. But for just a moment Nick's and Derrick's eyes connected, and for just a moment Nicholas saw something he had never seen in Derrick before—fear.

"STOP!"

Then they were gone. Out the door and down the street.

Nicholas and Louis looked at each other. Suddenly the store seemed to have lost its magic. The music carried no joy. Two of those kids—those thieves—were hoods old enough to be out of high school. And Derrick Cryder was with them.

But that didn't bother Nick as much as the look he had seen in Derrick's eyes. It had lasted only a split second—but in that split second Nick could have sworn Derrick's eyes seemed to shout, "Help me . . . I don't want to be here! I'm in over my head!"

Still, it wasn't Nick's business. I mean, he couldn't stand Derrick anyway. And Derrick certainly couldn't stand him. So it was Derrick's problem, not his.

At least that's what Nick wanted to think.

But from that moment on, something began to eat at Nicholas. He wasn't sure what it was or why it was there. But for whatever reason, Nicholas Martin could not put Derrick out of his mind.

Later that evening Nicholas's family celebrated their annual tree decorating time. Well, it was supposed to be tree decorating. But by the way Dad had tangled himself up in all the lights it looked more like Dad decorating. Sarah put it best when she referred to him as "the living Christmas tree."

"Hey, laugh all you want," he answered as he tried to fight his way through the cobweb of wires. "But as soon as I find the loose bulb on this puppy, you're all gonna need some shades."

Yeah, yeah, yeah, save the false bravado for someone who really knows how to bravado. Yes, it is I, Thomas McGee Edison, world-famous electrician and Oreo cookie connoisseur. Mr. Dad might look like he was fixing the lights, but I was the one who was really saving the day. I was engaging my incredibly ingenious electrical intelligence on the lightbulb problem when ol' Nicky boy spotted me at the base of the tree.

"Hey," he whispered. "You'd better be careful."

Careful, schmareful. I appreciated his concern, but he obviously didn't know whom he was addressing. "No pro-blem-o," I answered. *"What ya got here is a fused scattafrants with a polynine skrail blatz."*

171

"That's what I was gonna say," Nick said, trying his best to sound intelligent. Poor kid. Sometimes I feel sorry for him having to fake intelligence just to remain in my genius-like presence. But I guess that's the price you pay for hanging out with brilliance.

Still, being the sucker I am for intellectually underdeveloped folk, I let Nick take a gander over my shoulder. "I just reverse the gyro-stabilizers," I explained, "and connect them to these thinga-whatcha-majabbers, and . . ."

With one swift move I reached into the light socket and—ZZZZZZZZZ-BLUUUUUUUEEEEIIIIEEE!

Unfortunately, it wasn't the lightbulb that lit up. It was me! Talk about an electrifying experience! I was shocked! In more ways than one. In fact, if ol' Nicky boy hadn't pulled the plug I could have ended up with the most permanent poodle perm you've ever seen!

Fortunately I suffered no side effects from my enlightening experience. Well, almost none. Whenever I enter a room, there's still the minor problem of lightbulbs lighting up, automatic garage doors opening, and the channels on remote control TVs switching. But that's a small price to pay. Besides, it could just be because of my charged-up personality.

As McGee was once again delighting in his own greatness, Grandma swooped in from the kitchen with a tray of Christmas cookies.

"All right!" everyone shouted as they headed for the tray.

Well, almost everyone. It seems Dad was still a little tied up.

But his persistence paid off. Finally finding the missing

bulb, he shouted, "Here it is! OK, everybody, get ready. We're talking serious light show, now!"

Everyone stopped and turned. Somehow they suspected the worst. They loved and respected Dad. In fact, it seemed that everyone who knew him loved and respected him. He was a great guy, a great father, a great husband, and a great man of God. Unfortunately, he was not a great handyman.

With dramatic flair, he shoved the Christmas bulb into the socket. And with an equally dramatic flair, every light in the house went out.

The family groaned in unison.

"All right, not to worry," Dad called as he tried to fight his way through the wires. "I'll get the fuses. It will only take a—"

"No, don't, David." It was Mom. "This is kind of nice this way. You know, with the firelight and everything."

"Uh . . . right," Dad said, nervously clearing his throat. "I, uh, I planned it this way."

Of course everyone gave him a look and threw in another groan for good measure. And of course Dad pretended not to notice. I mean, after all, it was Christmas. If a guy couldn't get some slack from his family this time of year, when could he? "Here, Daddy," Sarah said as she handed him some popcorn. "Why don't you help me string these."

Dad looked dubiously at the tiny kernels of corn, the huge needle, and (most of all) the ultra sharp point at the end of the huge needle. But, being a man of extreme faith, he figured he'd give it a shot. "Sure," he said with a shrug, trying to remain casual. "Why not?"

The family could have thought of a million why nots, but hey, it was Christmas. If a guy couldn't get some slack from his family this time of year, when could he?

As Grandma sat beside Mom on the sofa she couldn't help commenting, "This is exactly how I remember Christmas as a little girl."

"No kidding?" Mom asked.

"Sure. The family all together, no electricity, just the light from the fire . . ." Then with a twinkle she added, "And popcorn fresh from the microwave."

Everyone gave a quiet chuckle. Well, almost everyone. Little sister Jamie was so intent on setting up the miniature nativity scene that she barely heard what the others were saying.

And then there was Nick. Try as he might, he just couldn't shake what he had seen in the store a few hours earlier. Oh sure, he was wrapping presents, decorating the tree, and laughing with everyone else. But that was on the outside. On the inside he was still thinking about Derrick Cryder. And on the outside he kept seeing that look of fear in Derrick's eyes.

Mom was the first to notice his mood. And, being the true-blue Mom that she is, she wanted to know what was going on. "Hey," she said quietly. "What's up?"

And Nick, being the true-blue kid that he is, gave the typical true-blue kid answer. "Nothin'."

Mom knew there was always something behind Nick's "nothin's," so she waited for more. Finally Nick continued.

"It's just kinda funny . . ." His voice trailed off for a second as he tried to piece his thoughts together. "Christmas is such a great time of year. Everywhere you look you can see, you know, people celebrating Christmas and stuff."

Mom nodded. So far, so good. But she knew there was more, and her continued silence asked, "So what's the problem?"

Nicholas knew what she wanted to know. So, after a long sigh, he continued. "It's just too bad everyone can't . . . enjoy it."

"But they can, honey," she gently corrected. "You know that. Christmas is what God's love is all about. Everyone can experience it."

Nicholas slowly looked up at her. That's what he had heard all his life. But that's not what he had seen that afternoon. In Derrick Cryder's eyes he saw nothing but hate and fear. He saw somebody who had no idea about God's love.

Mom kept insisting. "God's love is for everyone." She spotted the figures in Jamie's Nativity scene and motioned toward them. "Everyone from poor ragged shepherds to rich and powerful kings . . . to conniving thieves."

The last word shot into Nicholas's heart like an arrow. "Thieves?" he croaked. Once again he pictured the look in Derrick Cryder's eyes.

"Well, sure," Mom answered. "Remember the thief on the cross? How Jesus loved and forgave him?"

Nick's head began to spin. He knew God was supposed to love and forgive those who asked. He'd heard it a billion times . . . in church, in Sunday school, everywhere. But Derrick Cryder? The all-school hood? Derrick Cryder, the creepy bully who beat up everyone? Derrick Cryder, the . . . thief? A part of Nick knew it was supposed to be true. But a bigger part doubted it. A bigger part seemed to think Derrick was the exception—that even God could never love Derrick Cryder.

Before Nick could put all these thoughts into words, he was interrupted by a panicked little sister.

"Mom?" Jamie cried.

"What's the problem, hon?"

Desperately Jamie was plowing through the box in which the nativity characters had been packed. "I can't find the third wise man . . . I can't find him anywhere!"

"Oh, I'm sure he's in here somewhere," Mom said as she turned to comfort her.

Mom's comforting words did no good. By now little Jamie's chin was beginning to tremble, and her voice was sounding nervous and unsteady. "Maybe . . ." she swallowed hard to fight back the emotion. "Maybe he's . . . lost."

For the second time that evening Nick's heart felt as though it had suddenly been shot with an arrow. What about the third wise man in his pageant? Was he lost, too . . . ?

FOUR
Just When You Thought It Was Safe to Get Back on the Stage . . .

"Maybe I could sign up for the next dog-sled expedition to Antarctica. Or join a prison chain gang . . . or . . . or . . ." Mrs. Harmon muttered to herself, trying to think of some way to relax after directing this pageant. Something easier. Something peaceful.

"OK, Philip," she said, clapping her hands. "Let's try it one more time."

She'd said "one more time" about fifty times now. No matter how many times he tried, the tiny Santa just couldn't get out those "ho-ho-ho's."

Then there was Brutus. The giant dog had been on his best behavior. He'd been the perfect gentleman as they stuck the cardboard antlers onto his head. He'd been the model of obedience as they hooked him to the red wagon that was supposed to be Santa's sleigh.

Yes sir, everyone was proud of Brutus. Well, everyone but Fluffy, the little kitten that wanted to break into show biz. Every chance she got, cute little Fluffy would meow or growl or hiss at Brutus—anything she could think of to rile the poor guy. But Brutus was smarter than that. No way was he falling for any dumb old cat trick. The only problem was, Fluffy wasn't just any dumb old cat. . . .

Meanwhile, backstage, Louis got to be the bearer of some good tidings. "Hey, Nick," he called as he approached his friend. They were both dressed in their wise-man costumes (complete, of course, with sagging beards). But right now there were only two wise men. As promised, Derrick Cryder didn't show up. Now, normally, not having Derrick around would have brightened up Nicholas's day. But not after last night. Not after his talk with Mom. Not after he began to suspect that Derrick was in real trouble.

"Good news, bud," Louis continued. "Mrs. Harmon says we can bag the beards."

Nick grinned. It looked like rehearsal finally was starting to go right. Unfortunately, as he soon found out, looks can be deceiving.

"All right, let's try it one more time, Philip." Mrs. Harmon's voice sounded flat and dull, like she was on automatic pilot—like she really wasn't there. Maybe she wasn't.

Up on stage, the little Santa took a deep breath, stepped back into Brutus's wagon/sleigh, and tried again. Around him, all the other children were dressed as snowflakes, snowmen, Christmas gifts, Christmas trees, you name it—if it had something to do with Christmas, chances are somebody was dressed like it. Not only were they dressed like it, but they were standing around bored out of their minds. Even Brutus gave a loud yawn as he waited for Take 607 to begin.

But there was one critter who wasn't bored.

You guessed it: Fluffy.

Fluffy had a plan. That's right—cute, little, adorable,

innocent Fluffy was about to add more than a little spice to the rehearsal.

Philip cleared his throat and again attempted the introduction to the pageant . . .

"We're glad you came, you and the Mrs., to see Eastfield's pageant, 'Traditions of Christmas.'"

So far, so good. Mrs. Harmon found herself leaning closer. This was it. She crossed her fingers and silently mouthed the words with Philip. Any moment the "ho-ho-ho's" would come. Maybe, just maybe, he'd get them right.

"So sit back, relax, and enjoy our show, merry Christmas to all, and ho-ho-wooooAAAAAAAAAAAAA!!!!!!!"

Philip never got out that last ho, thanks to Fluffy, who had chosen that exact moment to make her move. In a flash she leaped out of the shepherdess's arms and jumped right into the middle of Brutus's back. She dug her claws in nice and deep, then took off and ran across the stage. No doubt she figured this would shake things up a bit.

She was right. Sort of. What it actually did was shake things down.

After letting out a tremendous howl of pain, Brutus did what any dog in his position would do. He raced after the cat. I guess he figured it was time for a little dog-to-cat talk. Maybe he was hoping they could sit down and chat over a nice long meal—with Fluffy as the main dish.

Actually, the dog chasing the cat wasn't the problem. It was the wagon that was attached to the dog that was chasing the cat.

And Philip. He'd never been to Disney World, but he

was sure that the ride he suddenly found himself on was just as good as any he'd find there. Or at least as scary.

First they shot across the stage to the left. Some children were screaming; others were laughing. Philip wasn't sure what he was doing. He may have been doing both. But one thing was certain . . . he was definitely hanging on. For dear life.

"AHHHHhhhhhhh!" he cried.

As they came to one end of the stage, Fluffy suddenly veered to the right and took off in the other direction. Brutus followed. So did the wagon. And so did Philip.

"OOOOOOoooooo!"

Now they were going the other way—full throttle. Fluffy was howling, Brutus was barking, and Philip . . . well, by now little Philip was definitely into his screaming mode.

"EEEEEeeeeeeee!"

Children jumped out of the way as the wagon swerved and crashed into anything in its path: props, trees, the manger. If it was on the stage, chances are it was hit by the wagon and sent flying through the air.

Then there were the dancing snowflakes. Philip was the first to see what was about to happen.

"Look out! . . . Watch it! . . . Get out of the way!!"

But the little girls just stood there, frozen. They didn't know which way to go. If they leaped to the right, Fluffy might turn in that direction. If they leaped to the left, Fluffy might head that way.

They didn't have to worry. Fluffy made the decision for them. She did another 180-degree turn and completely missed them. Brutus followed. Maybe the girls would be safe after all, maybe the wagon would also miss them, maybe there would be no catastrophe.

Then again, maybe not.

It was close, but not close enough. As the wagon swung around, it caught the leg of snowflake one. It didn't hit her hard, just hard enough to throw her off balance. Just hard enough to cause her to fall into snowflake two, who fell into snowflake three, who . . . well, suddenly it was a rerun of what happened the last rehearsal. The whole troop was falling like dominoes.

Unfortunately, that was only the beginning. When the last snowflake fell, she landed on one of the towering pieces of scenery at the edge of the stage. It was called a flat. And it was surrounded by several other flats just as tall.

Everyone looked up in terror as the flat started to tilt back. Then, as if trying to catch its balance, it leaned forward. Then back. A hush fell over the crowd as the tall flat continued to teeter back and forth, back and forth . . . and then it fell, directly into the flat behind it. Which fell into the flat behind it. Which fell into the flat behind it.

Once again it looked like someone was playing a giant game of Topple the Dominoes. Only this time, it wasn't dominoes or even snowflakes coming down—it was the entire set of the Christmas pageant.

Everyone watched in stunned horror as the set disintegrated before their eyes. Nicholas, Louis, Mrs. Harmon. Even little Fluffy—cute little Fluffy, who had hopped to safety onto a fire-hose box and was now calmly licking her paws—watched with a certain interest.

Finally the last flat fell with a mighty *K-THWUMP!*

Now everything was totally leveled. You could even see

the concrete wall at the back of the stage. For a long time it was very quiet. Then all eyes slowly turned to Mrs. Harmon.

"Well," she said, clearing her throat. "That was, uh . . . interesting." Then forcing her best smile she added, "All right, everybody, take five."

The crowd started to move off. But, realizing that it might take more than five minutes (more like five weeks) to fix the damage, Mrs. Harmon cleared her throat again. Everybody came to a stop. Now she was going to tell them the truth. Now, no matter how tough it was to take, she'd give it to them straight. "Ah . . . ," she stalled. Then suddenly forcing another grin, she said, "Better make that ten."

A few minutes later, Nick was hanging around backstage when he heard the following conversation.

"So you're telling me we have no third wise man?" It was Mrs. Harmon's voice. She was on the other side of the flat talking to the principal, Mr. Oliver.

Now, it's not like Nicholas was eavesdropping or anything like that. But when it's your teacher and your principal, and they're talking only three feet away, and you really want to hear what's going on . . . well, it's hard not to kind of overhear some of what's being said. In fact, it's hard not to kind of overhear every word.

"I didn't say he wouldn't be here for sure," Mr. Oliver corrected. "I just think you need to know Derrick is having some very serious problems at home right now."

"I'm sorry to hear that," Mrs. Harmon said. And you could tell by the tone of her voice that she really was sorry. Not for the sake of the pageant, either, but for Derrick.

182

Mr. Oliver let out a long sigh that seemed to say he was sorry, too. The two turned and started to walk away. As they walked, their conversation grew fainter and fainter.

But Nicholas had heard what he needed to hear. Derrick Cryder had ruined his day again. Only this time he hadn't done it by being a bully. This time he'd done it by being someone in need. Someone who, as his mother had pointed out, needed the love of the Lord.

It was Nicholas's turn to sigh. Why? Why, whenever he turned around, did he keep seeing Derrick in need? What was going on? Why couldn't he just get him out of his mind? I mean, it wasn't like Nick could do anything to help Derrick. The only help Nick had ever been to Derrick was to serve as his punching bag.

Still . . . Derrick seemed to be in Nick's thoughts constantly, along with the feeling that he should help. Somehow, some way, he should tell Derrick what his mom had said about God's love. He should let him know that whatever was going on, he didn't have to go it alone. But how? Nicholas wasn't Billy Graham. He was just a kid. Surely God would find someone else to talk to Derrick.

Wouldn't he?

"So what do you say, Bucko?"

Yes, it was I, the Thundering Thespian. I was still set on saving Nicky boy's little show. It had just taken longer than I had planned. Getting a new pair of wings drawn is no easy task. But here they were—right off the drawing board. I had flown over from the sketch pad in Nick's backpack with my new flappers, eager to show them off. But when I noticed my

183

pet protégé's furrowed brow, I knew he was pondering another ponderous problem.

"Nice flying," Nick mumbled, barely paying attention. "I hope this is a nonstop flight."

"No, no, I don't mean my flying—we know that's great— I mean Derrick. What are we going to do about Derrick?"

"I don't know," Nick groaned. "Maybe someone should talk to him. You know, find out what's wrong . . . that kinda thing."

I dipped to the right and made a perfect two-point landing right on Nicky boy's shoulder. You know the spot—the place in all those old cartoons where the "good conscience" speaks to the hero. I figured, hey, I'm wearing angel wings, why not give it a shot?

"What are you going to say to him?" I whispered quietly in his ear.

"Me!" Nicholas practically jumped. He hated it when I could read his mind like that. But, hey, as his very own cartoon creation and part time alter-ego, that came with the territory. "McGee," he continued, "what could I tell him?"

"I don't know," I said, starting to grin. "But it's Christmas. I bet you'll think of something."

"Look." Nick was already on his feet searching for excuses. "I don't . . . I don't even know where he is, OK?"

"Right," I agreed. "'Course you could always start off by checking his home."

Nicholas frowned again.

"No way! Go to his home? Absolutely not. No way, no how, are you ever going to see me at Derrick Cryder's home!"

I smiled, fluttered my wings, and took off for his sketch pad. "Sure thing, bub," I called. "Let me know when we get there. I still got a few feathers to preen."

184

FIVE
A Little House Call

Nick wasn't sure how he got to the apartment building where Derrick Cryder lived—or even exactly why he was there. All he knew was that it had something to do with what McGee had said, something to do with what his mom had said, and something to do with what God wanted.

Standing outside in the cold, Nick let out a long puff of white breath and watched as it drifted slowly above his head. This was stupid. Insane. Even if he saw Derrick, he wouldn't know what to say. In fact, if Derrick saw him, he wasn't sure he'd live long enough to say anything.

But he had gone this far, so he might as well finish it. Even if it was the last thing he ever did. Taking another deep breath, he reached for the lobby door and tugged it open. It gave a gritty screech. He slipped in and pulled it shut behind him as it gave another awful screech.

To call the room a lobby was an exaggeration. It was just a place with worn and chipped floor tiles and a couple of rows of little mailboxes stuffed into the wall. Everything was bathed in a weird yellow light. And the smells . . . they weren't completely suffocating, but they were definitely more lethal than just stale smoke and mildewing carpet.

Then there were the sounds. A baby crying at the top of his lungs. An older guy shouting and yelling in an apartment down the hall. But just a couple of doors away someone was playing "Silent Night." It was kind of pretty. And in a place like this, it was more than a little comforting.

Right next to the mailboxes, Nick spotted the directory. It was inside a glass case. White letters on a black board. Well, it used to be black. Now a good portion of it was starting to fade and turn brown from the sun.

Nicholas took a step closer. "Albert, Anderson, Brenner . . ." His mittened hand carefully followed the names down the directory. "Campbell, Cramer, Cryder . . ." There it was. Cryder—apartment 6.

Suddenly, before Nick had a chance to turn and head for what he feared might be his doom, the yelling down the hall grew louder. It was followed by a loud slap and then a muffled cry.

Nick turned just in time to see an apartment door open and a boy rush out, holding his cheek and whimpering. Quickly Nick sucked in his breath. It was Derrick Cryder!

Derrick slammed the door and started down the hall . . . directly toward Nicholas!

At first Nick thought of running, of throwing open the lobby door and racing for his life. But everything was too strange. Derrick Cryder crying? Then, before he had a chance to get his bearings, it was too late. Before he knew it, Derrick looked his way and their eyes met.

There was a moment of shock for both of them. And

186

embarrassment. Then Derrick gave his eyes a quick swipe, dropped into his famous I'm-a-too-tough-dude slouch, and demanded in a rough voice, "What are you doing here?"

It almost worked. Derrick was almost able to become the Derrick everyone knew and feared. Almost, but not quite. Maybe it was the way his voice cracked. Or maybe it was the look in his eyes—that same look Nicholas had seen in the gift shop. A look of fear and hurt.

But it lasted only a second. Immediately Derrick pulled back into the shadows of the hallway so Nick couldn't see him well. But that was OK. Nick wasn't looking. Instinctively he had focused on the chipped tile at his feet. He had seen a Derrick Cryder he was sure no one else at school had seen. And suddenly, surprisingly, Nick wanted to be careful not to embarrass Derrick any further.

"I said," Derrick demanded as his voice grew stronger, "what are you doing here, squid?"

Well, here goes, Nick thought. *It's now or never.* He opened his mouth. At first nothing came out. He swallowed and tried again. At last a few words started to come.

"Look, I uh . . . umm . . . uh. . . ." Well, only a few words. He cleared his throat and tried again. "That is, uh, we . . . well, we, you know, we missed you."

There! At last he found a handle. Some place to start. Now if he could just go on from there! "Yeah," he croaked, growing in confidence. "We missed you at rehearsal today, and I just stopped by on my way home to—"

Now he was on a roll. Now he was able to look up at

Derrick and . . . oops. He shouldn't have done that. Look up at Derrick, I mean. Because the expression on Derrick's face said he wasn't buying it—any of it. Since when had anyone ever missed him? Since when was anybody ever sorry that he, Derrick Cryder, wasn't around?

Nicholas swallowed again, though by now his mouth was so dry he had little left to swallow. Suddenly, there was a muffled roar of a car approaching outside. Both boys threw a glance toward the street. A dark, souped-up Mustang, missing more than its fair share of paint, rumbled to a stop at the curb. Nick didn't recognize it, but by the tension he saw cross Derrick's face, he knew Derrick did.

Nick took another breath and tried again. It didn't look like he had much time, and he'd better say what he'd come to say . . . whatever it was.

"OK, well, maybe that's not the reason. Well, OK, it's part of the reason, but really, uh, I mean, that is . . ." Enough small talk. Finally it was time to lay it all out on the table. It was tough, but it was what Nicholas really felt. "Derrick, are you all right?"

The sincerity in Nick's voice caught Derrick off guard. But before he had a chance to answer, the Mustang's horn began to blast. Now his attention was split between Nicholas and the Mustang. "What are you really doing here?" he demanded.

Again Nicholas tried to swallow. And again he tried to explain. "It's Christmas." It wasn't much of an explanation, but it was all he had.

"What?"

The horn continued to blast.

"You know, Christmas." Nicholas started fumbling again. "It's supposed to be a time to care about other people, and, uh . . ." He looked at Cryder and again he lost his train of thought.

The horn blasted.

Nick tried again. He was going to get through this if it killed him. "I mean, that's the whole reason for Christmas in the first place . . . right?" Things were getting worse, and he knew it. Not only was his voice getting weaker, but the horn was blasting louder, and Nick doubted he was making any sense at all.

By the look on Derrick's face he knew he was right about the last part. Still, he pressed on. "You know, uh, 'cause God loved us . . . and all that . . ."

He was failing miserably.

". . . sort of . . ."

He was barely making sense, even to himself. Finally the last word came out. But it was more a squeak than a word.

". . . stuff."

There, he'd said it. Maybe it didn't make any sense, but at least he'd said it.

It was no surprise that Derrick looked puzzled and confused. But he also looked like he might have understood . . . just a little. Nicholas wasn't sure.

He never found out. The lobby door suddenly flew open, and there stood Derrick's older friend—the one in the leather jacket that had ripped off the stuff from the gift shop. The blast of cold air from the outside made Nicholas shudder. Then again, maybe it wasn't the cold air. . . .

189

"Let's go, Cryder!" the kid shouted. "We haven't got all night!"

For a moment Derrick also seemed to shudder—and it wasn't because of the cold either. It was because of the menacing grin the boy was wearing, the menacing grin directed right at Nicholas.

"Well, well, well, who do we have here?" The older boy sauntered up to Nick. He was almost a foot taller and probably forty pounds heavier. That wasn't the problem, though. The problem was what Nicholas was wearing.

Now, Nick's not rich. Not by a long shot. But his mom works pretty hard to help the kids look their best—even without much money. Unfortunately, it was this looking their best that had suddenly become Nick's problem. Maybe it was the scarf, or the stocking hat, or even the new mittens. Whatever it was, when the older kid saw Nicholas, his face showed what he was thinking: "Spoiled, rich brat." And that definitely meant Nicholas had a problem.

"So . . . ," the kid sneered in Derrick's direction. "You plan on bringing your pet freak along tonight?"

Derrick tried his best to be cool. But you could tell by the way his eyes darted around that he knew this kid could be trouble . . . real trouble. "Look, uh . . ." Derrick cleared his throat and motioned toward Nicholas. "He's just a twerp from that stupid play I'm in."

"What?" The kid sounded angry.

Derrick decided to play it safe and bail. "I'm not in it anymore!" he quickly added. "I quit."

For just the slightest second it looked like the kid's face relaxed.

190

"Come on," Derrick encouraged, "let's get out of here."

But the kid wasn't ready to go. Not just yet. He reached down to the costume Nick was still holding under his arm—the robe and turban from the pageant. Still sneering, he half whispered, half hissed, "Nice dress, girlie."

Nick was paralyzed with fear.

Derrick began to fidget nervously. "Ray . . ."

So the kid's name was Ray. A nice, simple name, Nicholas thought. Straight, to the point, and yet with a certain flair. The type of flair that could spell real disaster.

The sneer slowly disappeared from Ray's face.

Great, Nicholas thought.

But not so great. The sneer was turning into a scowl. Slowly Ray leaned into Nick's face. Not more than four inches separated them. In fact, if Nicholas had been breathing, he would have noticed it'd been awhile since the kid had brushed his teeth. But Nick wasn't breathing. In fact, he wasn't doing much of anything . . . except praying.

"I don't know who your friend is," Ray continued to hiss. He was talking to Derrick, but by the glare he was drilling into Nicholas's head, it was pretty obvious he was really addressing him. "But you tell him if I see his spoiled rich face on this side of town again, I'm going to have to kick it all the way back to where it belongs. You got that?"

Both boys got it . . . loud and clear.

"Yeah, yeah," Derrick answered nervously. "Now, come on, let's get out of here before my dad comes."

But Ray was in no hurry. He wanted to make sure he'd put the proper fear into the spoiled rich kid. The look on

Nick's face said he had succeeded. He'd succeeded big time!

Just then the horn blasted again, and Ray broke back into that little sneer of his. Nicholas never thought he'd be happy to see it. But that little sneer was better than the scowl. A thousand times better.

Suddenly Ray reached his hand up to Nick's cheek and gave it a little pinch, then a gentle slap. "Ciao," he said with a smirk. Then, to add further insult—"Chicken."

At the moment Nicholas didn't mind the insult. He figured being a live chicken was a lot better than a dead hero.

In an instant Ray turned and threw open the lobby door. Derrick followed without a word. But just before he disappeared out the door he turned back to Nicholas.

"Listen . . . Martin . . ."

The two stood still for just a moment, neither of them sure what Derrick was going to say. Maybe he wasn't going to say anything. But then again . . .

The horn honked and, again, there was Ray's voice: "C'mon, Cryder!"

Derrick turned and headed out the door into the night. Nicholas watched as the boy got into the backseat of the Mustang with Ray and another kid, and then they squealed off.

Suddenly everything was very quiet.

It had started to snow again.

Nicholas stood in the silence for a long moment. He was stunned and awed by how still everything had become—almost as if the last five minutes had never happened.

192

There was no other sound, no other movement—just the falling snow. Oh, and one other thing. From down the hall, just a few doors away, came the ending strains to the Christmas carol that had been playing. The music was soft and faint, but there was no missing the final words:

"Sleep in heavenly peee-eeace. . . . Slee-eep in heavenly peace."

SIX
Opening Fright

Finally it was Christmas Eve. Great!

Of course, that meant it also was the night of the big show. Not so great.

To be honest, Nick really wasn't too worried. The fact that he had rehearsed his lines all afternoon in front of the hallway mirror, well, that was just good preparation. The fact that he had spent almost an hour in the shower, well, that was just good hygiene. And the fact that he had completely shellacked his hair with hair spray and used half a bottle of Dad's after-shave . . . well, you never know when a Hollywood talent agent might drop in.

"Let's move, we're going to be late!" Dad hollered for about the tenth time. And for about the tenth time nobody paid attention. How could they? Not when there was still eyeshadow, lipstick, and of course more hair spray to put on.

For years everyone had known that "Let's-move-we're-going-to-be-late!" was just the first warning. Things weren't critical yet. Not by a long shot. There were still two more warnings to come.

Next would be the famous "I'm not kidding! We have to go!" When you heard that, you knew it was getting close. Still, you'd probably have time to try on a couple more pairs of shoes or, if you were lucky, to slip on one last dress.

It was only when they heard "All right, everyone! We're going, and we're going now!" that the family knew Dad really meant business. There would be no messing around after those words. Once you heard those words you were either heading for the car or staying home.

"I'm not kidding! We have to go!" Ah, the second warning. But for once Nick didn't need a second warning. He already was heading down the stairs to join his dad in the kitchen. In fact, Nicholas had been dressed and bathed and sprayed and combed and ready to go for nearly two hours now. Surely this was further evidence that he wasn't nervous. Petrified, maybe. But not nervous.

Grandma was next to make her appearance. She came down the steps wearing a long dark skirt, a gorgeous white sweater, and a single strand of pearls around her neck.

"Whew! Look at you!" Dad said with appreciation.

Grandma gave a regal nod to her adoring subjects. "So how do you feel, Nick?" she asked. "A little nervous?"

"Naw," Nick said with a shrug. Then, seeing his dad open his mouth, he thought he'd try to beat him to the punch line. But no such luck. "A lot nervous," they said in unison.

Finally Dad turned toward the stairs to call out his third and last warning. "All right, everyone! We're going, and we're going now!"

Immediately there was a loud stampede upstairs. It sounded like a herd of wild buffalo—but it looked like

Sarah, Mom, and little Jamie charging down the stairs at the same time. Dad threw Nick a grin. Did he know how to get his family in gear or what?

The three reached the bottom of the steps and raced for the coatrack, where they threw on their hats, coats, and scarfs. Dad was still smiling as he opened the door and watched his herd gallop past.

As Jamie moved by, she stuck something out for her brother.

"What's this?" Nicholas asked.

"If you really mess up, you can wear it home."

Nicholas carefully unfolded it. It was a ski mask! What a comfort to know his little sister had such confidence in him.

By the time the family arrived at the auditorium, most of the best seats were already taken. With a little luck (and the fact that most of the ushers were guys who had a crush on Sarah), the Martins managed to find a few good seats in the middle section. Of course, there were the usual hassles of sitting in the middle . . . like climbing over a million and a half feet. But finally they were all seated and ready for the show.

Well, almost. It seems Dad had forgotten something. "I'll be right back," he said as he rose to his feet. Of course, everyone was a little put out as, once again, he had to crawl all over those million and a half feet.

But Dad had to go backstage and tell Nicholas something very important. . . .

Backstage was a zoo. Literally! Everywhere you looked there were either live animals, stuffed animals, or people dressed up like animals. In fact, when Dad first poked his head around the flat, it looked more like Noah's ark than the birth of Christ. At last he found his son and called to him.

"Nicholas!"

Nick was standing beside Louis. Both boys were in their wise-man costumes. There was no sign of the third wise man.

"Nicholas!" This time Dad called a little louder.

"Oh," Nick answered. "Hi, Dad." Both Nick and Louis crossed toward him to see what was up.

"Listen," Dad said, pouring a small handful of quarters into Nick's hands. "Here's your allowance. Now everything's set. After the performance I'll take the rest of the family over for some yogurt. That way you can go out and get the music box for Mom. She'll never know a thing. But come straight home."

Nicholas eagerly accepted the money and broke into a grin. With the worries of the pageant and Derrick Cryder, he'd almost forgotten about the music box. "Sure thing," he said, beaming. "Thanks!"

Dad nodded and started back toward the auditorium. Then, remembering his manners, he turned and hoarsely whispered, "Break a leg, you guys!"

Louis spun around in concern. "What?" But he was already gone.

"Break a leg," Nick repeated.

Louis still didn't get it.

"In the theater it means, like, 'good luck.'"

"In this show," Louis sighed, "it's, like, a possibility."

"All right, places everybody . . . places." It was Mrs.

Harmon, once again doing what she did best—clapping and pretending to be happy. But if you looked closely into her eyes, you could see that maybe, just maybe, Louis had a point.

A hush fell over the audience as the lights dimmed. The way everybody leaned forward in their seats you would have thought it was opening night on Broadway. Of course, those were parents in those seats. And it was their children up on that stage. So, in many ways, it was more important than any Broadway opening night.

The spotlight came up and focused on little Philip, nervously standing in his sleigh. He was holding the reins to Brutus, the red-nosed dogdeer, and he was looking more than a little frightened. But old Brutus wasn't going anywhere. And, whether he knew it or not, little Philip was about to give the performance of his life.

With a deep breath he began. . . .

"We're glad you came, you and the Mrs., to see Eastfield's pageant, 'Traditions of Christmas.'"

So far, so good. But now came the tricky part. As Mrs. Harmon watched from backstage, she crossed her fingers, her toes, her legs, and anything else there was left to cross.

Suddenly there was a commotion behind her. She turned and spotted Derrick Cryder arriving . . . complete with his robe and turban. Without a word he moved past her to join the other two wise men who were standing in the Nativity scene, waiting for the curtain to rise.

"Glad you could make it," Mrs. Harmon whispered as he passed.

Without missing a beat he answered, "Somebody said you're giving fewer quizzes the rest of the semester."

Mrs. Harmon had to smile. She knew exactly what he meant. She had blackmailed him by threatening to flunk him. Now he was blackmailing her by showing up! The kid obviously had a future in big business.

Nick watched with pleasure as Derrick joined him. For the first time he could remember, Nicholas was actually happy to see Derrick. He wanted to say this, to tell Derrick how glad he was that he made it . . . but he didn't say a word. It would have only embarrassed and angered Derrick. It would have only gone against his code of ultra-cool-hood.

Instead, both boys prepared themselves for their entrance. The curtain was about to rise. Little Philip was already in the second part of his speech . . . the critical part . . .

"So sit back, relax, and enjoy our show, merry Christmas to all, and ho-ho-ho!"

With that, the little guy gave Brutus's reins a flick, and the megadog trotted off as gentle as you please.

It was perfect! Wonderful! Sensational! And the audience didn't hesitate to show their approval. Immediately they broke into cheers as the little boy and the big dog with cardboard antlers headed off.

Now it was time for the Nativity scene.

The curtain slowly rose, and the audience grew very quiet. There before them was one of the most beautiful nativities they had ever seen. Everything was there: the stable, the animals, the shepherds, the three wise men, Joseph and Mary, and, of course, the manger, where the baby Jesus lay.

But it was more than just the scenery and actors that made the moment so special. There was something else.

As everybody on stage and in that auditorium turned their attention to the tiny crib, a gentle sense of awe and wonder began to ripple through them.

For a moment—just a moment—they really thought about Christmas, what it means. Sure, it is a time of Santa Clauses and reindeer, Christmas pageants and Christmas gifts, tree decorating and snowflakes (dancing or otherwise). But slowly it dawned on everyone in that auditorium that Christmas is a season of something more . . . of something greater.

A soft spotlight came up on the stage, and Nicholas quietly stepped forward. He was about to deliver his lines. Like the scene itself, the lines suddenly took on a deeper meaning. They were more than just words now. They were the whole reason for the evening—the whole reason for Christmas. . . .

"That night some shepherds were in the fields outside the village, guarding their flocks of sheep."

Nick's voice was strong and steady. He stumbled over an occasional word, but nobody seemed to care. Everyone was more interested in what he was saying than in how he was saying it.

"Suddenly an angel appeared among them, and the landscape shone bright with the glory of the Lord. They were badly frightened."

There wasn't a sound in the auditorium. It was as if everyone was watching and listening to the story for the very first time. Maybe some of them were.

"But the angel reassured them. 'Don't be afraid!' he said. 'I bring you the most joyful news ever announced, and it is for everyone!

"'The Savior—yes, the Messiah, the Lord—has been born tonight in Bethlehem! How will you recognize him? You will find a baby wrapped in a blanket, lying in a manger!' Suddenly, the angel was joined by a vast host of others—the armies of heaven—praising God:

"'Glory to God in the highest heaven,' they sang, 'and peace on earth for all those pleasing him.'"

Nick practically shouted the last few lines. It was true. Not only had Jesus come to save people, but he also came to give them peace. Not peace from wars and battles . . . but a peace inside their hearts, a peace deep inside where it really counted, a peace available to everyone . . . "For *all* those pleasing him"!

Everybody was moved by that last phrase. Especially Derrick. It really seemed to touch him. I mean, if there was anyone who needed peace—if there was anyone who needed to know he was loved—it was Derrick Cryder.

That probably was why, as Nick turned to walk back to his place, he clearly saw Derrick reaching up and brushing a tear from his eye.

SEVEN
Confrontation

Two hours later Nick was standing inside the little gift shop. The sign on the door said Closed, but the shopkeeper had been listening for Nicholas's knock.

It had been a perfect night. Philip had been perfect. Brutus had been perfect. In fact, the whole pageant had been perfect. Then, to top it off, Derrick Cryder had shown up! It couldn't get much more perfect.

Now the shopkeeper was behind the counter. Once again she was lifting the music box from the shelf and setting it before him. Only this time it would never return to the shelf. This time it was going home to Nicholas's mom.

Carefully he ran his hand over the intricate carvings of the glass lid. Gently he opened it and listened as the box began to play. The chiming of the "Carol of the Bells" was just as haunting and stirring as ever. Nicholas looked up to the weathered old lady and grinned.

"I'll get you a box," she said, smiling.

Yes, it was a perfect Christmas.

Not far away, in a dark alley, a hand suddenly grabbed Derrick by the shirt and threw him against a cyclone fence. The fence rattled loudly, which set a couple of dogs barking.

"Where were you?" The snarled question came from Ray, Derrick's "friend." Ray and one of his pals towered menacingly over Derrick. They were lit only by the Mustang's headlights as it idled noisily nearby.

Derrick tried to move, but Ray pinned him hard against the fence. "You know we needed a twerp to squeeze under the gate of that warehouse!"

"I was, uh . . ." Derrick tried to stay cool, but with little success.

"Hey, look at this!" the other kid shouted.

Derrick froze.

They had spotted his costume from the pageant lying on the ground. It had fallen out of his arms when Ray had thrown him against the fence.

The sneer on Ray's face grew deeper. Now he knew where Derrick had been. "You were play-acting with your stinkin' rich friend, weren't you?"

"I, uh . . ."

"Weren't you?" His hold on Derrick grew tighter. So tight the boy could barely breathe. Derrick tried to explain, but all that came out were gargled gasps.

Ray pressed harder. *"Weren't you?"*

Finally Derrick nodded. That was all it took. With one powerful move Ray threw him across the alley—slamming him hard against a garbage dumpster. The dogs barked louder.

"Listen, slime!" Ray was breathing hard now. In the cold air, his breath spewed in great white plumes. "I let you tag along, even though you're just a dumb punk. But now, after hanging around that little geek, you think you're too good for us. Is that it?"

"Ra—"

"*Is that it?*"

Once again Ray grabbed Derrick and jerked him to his feet. Only this time he flung him several feet into the air. Derrick landed hard on the Mustang's fender. He gave a loud "Ommph" as all the air rushed from his lungs. But he had no time to feel the pain. Ray was coming at him slowly, and by the look on his face it would be for the last time. . . .

"Ray," he croaked.

"Go on. Get outta here." Ray's voice was low and quivering. He meant business. "Get outta my sight."

Derrick scrambled to his feet.

"I said, get outta here!"

Derrick needed no further invitation. Immediately he turned and stumbled down the alley.

"But if I see you or that punk friend of yours again . . . you're history!"

The last words echoed up and down the alley as Derrick rounded the corner and headed out into the street.

For the last time, Nicholas heard the little bell above the shop door jingle as he closed it. It was colder outside than he remembered, but it was also more beautiful. Somehow the chill made everything more vivid, more alive. The street decorations seemed to twinkle more brightly. The carolers a few doors down sang more cheerfully. Even the bell from the Salvation Army Santa across the street rang more clearly.

All that, and it was starting to snow again.

Yes, it was a perfect Christmas Eve. The most perfect ever.

Nicholas carefully stuffed the treasured gift under his arm, adjusted his scarf, and started on his way. Inside his head he could still hear the melody from the music box. Already he could see the look on his mother's face when she opened it. She'd be smiling, of course. But there would also be tears. Even that would be perfect.

The cassette player throbbed as Ray's partner swung the car onto the street. Ray was still angry. Real angry. What business did Derrick have hanging out with rich kids, anyway? They could have made good money by hitting that warehouse. But no, Derrick had to be in some stupid play with some rich brat.

Ray hated anyone who was, or appeared to be, rich. He was sure that everything he never had somehow had gone to them. He couldn't prove it, but all that money and all that "good life" had to go somewhere. And since he always had so little and they always had so much . . .

That was OK, though. Ray would show them. He would show them all.

Nicholas turned the corner and headed for home. It was still snowing and the "Carol of the Bells" was still chiming merrily inside his head.

Half a block away, the Mustang's headlights caught the unmistakable form of Nicholas Martin, bouncing for home. Ray was the first to spot him. "Well, well, well," he said in a soft, dangerous voice, "what do we have here?"

"Turn right," Ray quietly growled to his friend. "Circle around."

The driver punched the gas, and the Mustang squealed off around the corner.

Nicholas continued down the street. In less than twenty minutes, the family would all start to open their presents. Soon his mom would be opening the best gift he had ever given. Of course, he'd be receiving gifts, too. But somehow, for Nicholas, this year the receiving wasn't quite as important as the giving.

In the next alley, not more than fifty feet ahead of Nicholas, the driver shut off the Mustang's engine and turned out its lights. Now there was only the sound of crunching gravel as the dark machine coasted to a stop.

The door opened. There was no missing the distinct form of Ray's leather jacket as he quietly shut the door and headed off.

Nick was thinking of Derrick. He had failed in trying to tell Derrick about Christmas and God's love and everything. He had failed miserably. But for some reason the guy had still showed up at the pageant. Why? Maybe it was Mrs. Harmon's threat about flunking him. Still . . . And what about that tear Nicholas had seen in Derrick's eye when he had finished his speech?

That had to mean something.

Without a sound Ray pressed against the wall. He had found a place where the shadows were so dark and so deep that he could completely disappear into them. Only the white clouds of breath above his head gave away his presence. His breathing was slow and controlled. He knew exactly what he would do. Nicholas was less than fifteen feet away.

For a second Nicholas slowed. The prized gift he had kept under his arm was starting to slip. He quickly took it in his other hand and started off again.

Then it happened.

Suddenly Nick was yanked into the darkness. Suddenly and violently. Before he could yell, before he even knew what hit him, he was sailing through a black void. He landed in what felt like a heap of boxes. But it wasn't the boxes that hurt. It was the hard metal garbage cans under those boxes. In an instant he and the cans went clattering to the ground. And, in an instant, Nicholas's head hit the pavement . . . hard.

But just before he landed, almost as though in a dream, he caught sight of the music box as it flew from his hands. In slow motion he saw it sliding across the frozen asphalt. He heard the sickening sound of wood and glass scraping against gravel and pavement.

And then he hit.

It still seemed like a dream—or like he was floating underwater and the music box was playing above him somewhere, soft and muffled. Then the sound grew sharper . . . along with the pounding in his head. The music box *was* playing. Only it was playing somewhere in the alley. Somewhere in that cold, frozen night it was chiming out its haunting little melody.

Nicholas lay stunned. He still wasn't entirely sure where he was or what had happened. Then he saw it . . .

208

a large, dark form. It was moving. And it was moving toward him. It was impossible to make out who it was. There was only the silhouette of a large boy wearing a large leather jacket.

Nick tried to move, to get his bearings. But he couldn't find his legs. Everything was still too weak and blurry. He tried to call out, to say something, anything. But no words would come.

The silhouetted form was much closer now. Giant puffs of white breath were billowing from its mouth.

And then he spoke. "How was the play, girlie?"

Nicholas froze, a shock of terror jolting though him. Even in his bleary state, he recognized the voice—and it sounded meaner and more menacing than ever before.

Again Nick tried to move, but his legs would not obey.

Now the hulking form was nearly on top of him, and Nick heard a vicious little chuckle as two large hands reached out to grab him, bunching Nick's coat collar around his neck—

Suddenly, from out of the blue, another form appeared. It smashed into the first as if shot from a cannon. Together the two shadows tumbled onto the frozen asphalt with grunts and cries of pain. Then they began to slug it out.

Nick tried to rise for a better look. But it felt like a giant ball bearing was inside his head, crashing into the sides of his skull whenever he tried to move. Then there were his legs. They were no closer to obeying his commands than before. All he could do was watch the flurry of fists and legs.

The groans and cursings and stifled yells grew louder.

Whoever this newcomer was, he certainly was giving Ray a run for his money. Suddenly the shadows were up. But only for a second before they fell back down, skidding painfully across the gritty pavement. Bloody knees and elbows pumped and kicked.

"Hey! You there!" It was a voice of a neighbor, a passerby. But the forms ignored it.

"I'm calling the cops!"

As quickly as the fight had started, it was over. A torn and ragged Ray slowly rose over his victim. Apparently he had won, but by the swelling and cuts across his face, it looked like it had been close. He hovered over his defeated opponent a moment, swaying unsteadily. Then he spat on the ground, turned, and staggered down the alley.

Nick watched as Ray's silhouette disappeared. The Mustang roared to life, was thrown into reverse, and squealed backward out of the alley.

Suddenly everything grew quiet. The only sound was the music box as its fragile melody slowly wound down.

With the greatest of effort, and despite the ball bearing still crashing in his head, Nicholas finally managed to sit up and focus his eyes. It was difficult to see because of the shadows—and because of his cut and swollen face. But there, lying on the ground not ten feet away from him, was Derrick Cryder.

Derrick slowly began to stir to life. Groaning slightly, he lifted himself up on his elbows and looked at Nick. For a moment, the boys looked at each other—neither one entirely certain what had happened.

And somewhere nearby, the music finally stopped.

EIGHT
New Beginnings

"And when I saw him thumpin' on the Squid—er . . . Nick, here, I mean—before I knew it, I was in there punching away."

The Martin car cut through the thin layer of snow that had accumulated on the hospital parking lot. To be safe, Mom and Dad had thought it best to have both boys checked out at the E.R. But after X rays, a little poking, and a little probing, the doctor said everything was OK. Except for a few bruises and a couple gashes, everything was just fine.

At first, when they got the phone call, the folks had had quite a scare. But now everything was settling back to normal. Well, as normal as Nick's life ever got. Right now, both Nick and Derrick were in the backseat, reliving what had happened . . . for the umpteenth time. And each time the story got a little bigger and a little better.

"But the neatest thing is," Nicholas exclaimed, "Derrick never would have done that for me before. I mean, stepping in and helping like that."

"No way," Derrick agreed. "I wouldn't have done that for nobody."

There was a moment of silence as both boys digested this cold, hard truth.

"The weird thing is," Derrick finally continued, "I really don't know why I did it this time. It's like . . ." Again he fell silent for a moment as he tried to figure it out. "It's like something's happening." Another long moment passed. At last he gave a shrug. "I don't get it. I don't get any of it."

In the front seat Mom and Dad exchanged glances. For months they had heard about Derrick Cryder, and for months they had told Nick there was hope for anyone, even Derrick.

Dad was the first to speak. "It sounds like you're starting to go through some changes."

Derrick glanced up at him. The man was right. Of course, Derrick was too cool to admit it. But the look on his face said he wanted to hear more—lots more. Dad obliged.

"And not just you," he continued. "I mean, the same thing happened with Nick. I bet the last thing in the world he wanted to do was to visit your place the other night."

"Boy, you got that right," Nicholas agreed, perhaps a little too quickly.

Derrick shot him a look. It was Nicholas's turn to give a shrug. Hey, at least he was being honest.

"But," Dad continued, "there was something stronger at work than just what you two wanted."

Now he had both boys' interest. It was true—neither one of them really wanted to do what he did. I mean, going to Derrick's apartment was certainly not Nick's idea of a good time. And Derrick could have thought of a hundred better things to do than getting creamed by Ray just to save Nick's neck. And yet, somehow, they both wound up doing the harder thing—the better thing. Why?

"It's love," Mom finally said. "God's love."

Normally Derrick would have scoffed at the idea. But after tonight, well, who knew? Anything was possible. So instead of scoffing, Derrick just listened.

Mom and Dad carefully began to explain to Derrick how much God really loved him—how much he really loved everyone. They described how God wanted to be our friend, but how we've all turned our backs on him and disobeyed. Then, even more carefully, they explained how Jesus came to earth to take the punishment for that disobedience.

"You mean this Jesus guy got beat up, and spit on, and killed . . . just so he could take the rap for all my crumminess?" Derrick asked.

"You got it," Dad said.

"Everything?"

"Everything."

"So . . . what's in it for him?"

"Not a thing."

Derrick whistled. This was getting interesting.

"The only thing he wants," Mom added, "is to be your Boss and your Friend."

"Yeah, right," Derrick smirked. "Me, friends with God."

"Why not?" she challenged.

Derrick looked at her in surprise. This *was* getting interesting. Why not, indeed?

213

"'Cuz . . . well, well, I'm just not good enough," Derrick finally stuttered.

"None of us are," Mom said.

Then, almost before he knew it, Nick had his mouth open. Normally he wouldn't have much to say on the subject. I mean, Jesus and God and all that—it was hard stuff to talk about. Especially to someone who's been spending the school year making your life miserable. Yet he and Derrick had been through so much together, and, well . . . it sure looked like God had gone out of his way to bring Derrick this far. The least Nick could do was to give him a little hand.

"That's the whole reason Jesus came," he began. "Because we're not good enough."

Derrick turned to him a little surprised. But Nicholas was on a roll and wasn't stopping.

"You see, it doesn't matter how good a person is or how often they go to church or anything like that. It's whether or not they want Jesus to take the blame for all the wrong they've done."

"Well, who wouldn't?" Derrick challenged.

"Got me," Nick agreed. "It'd be pretty stupid not to."

"Real stupid," Derrick said. "But if a person did that, wouldn't they have to start, like you said, letting him be their Boss and doing good and stuff?"

"That's true." It was Dad's turn to answer. "But letting God be your Boss and doing good, that would all start coming naturally—as naturally as your stepping into that fight to save Nicholas."

A silence fell over the car as the four drove through the night. Derrick was obviously thinking, and thinking hard.

214

So was Nicholas. He had never talked to anyone so boldly about Jesus. He had never asked anyone if he wanted to become a Christian. But there was a first time for everything.

Another long moment passed. Then, finally, after taking a moment to find his voice, Nicholas asked the question. It wasn't loud, and, to be honest, it really wasn't all that bold. In fact, it was kind of shaky. But it was still being asked.

"Derrick . . . is this, like, something you might want? You know, to be friends with God and stuff?"

Derrick turned to him. The two looked at each other for a long moment.

NINE
Wrapping Up

Yes-siree-bob. Ol' Nicky boy was right. It was one perfect Christmas. But it wasn't perfect because of the snow, or the pageant, or even because of all the neato-keen gifts I managed to haul in.

That Christmas was perfect because Derrick and Nick both got another kind of gift. A real gift. The gift of God's love. Derrick's gift came when he decided he did want to be friends with God, to let God be his Boss. And Nicholas's gift was that God used him to help give Derrick his gift. So, if you ask me, both of the guys won, and in a big way. It's like I always say— that's what Christmas is really all about . . . God giving us his greatest gift: his Son, Jesus Christ.

Of course, the Martins invited Derrick home that Christmas Eve. And, of course, Derrick refused. He had too much to think over. I mean, let's face it, the guy had made a pretty big decision. But he promised he would swing by the house some- time before school started up. After all, he had questions. Lots of 'em.

And, just in case you were wondering, Nick managed to retrieve Mrs. Mom's music box. It was pretty chipped and scratched by the time he gave it to her. But somehow those chips and scratches made it all the more valuable.

"Oh, Nicholas," she said as she took it in her hands.

But that was all she got out before the waterworks started. And we ain't talking small-time sniffles, either. I mean, you would've guessed we'd sprung a water main, the way the tears were flowin'.

Then, when she opened the lid and the music started playing . . . well, you could kiss any dry eye in the house good-bye. Everybody was getting into the act. Even yours truly.

"What's goin' on?" I finally managed to sniff between bawling attacks. "Somebody peelin' onions around here?"

But before Nick could give me one of his snappy comebacks, ol' Mom had thrown a lovelock around him so tight he could barely breathe. Then, before you knew it, the whole family joined in. Suddenly I was swept up into this giant hug-in. I couldn't move, I couldn't talk. And pretty soon I could feel my colors starting to rub off on their clothes.

Oh well, there are probably worse ways for a cartoon character to go than being hugged to death.

And speaking of going . . . I see by the giant watch being scrunched into my face from Mr. Dad's arm that it's time to split. So, good tidings, good cheer, ta-ta, and Merry Christmas! (Unless of course you happen to be reading this in February, when it's Happy Valentine's Day . . . or in April, Happy Easter . . . or in May, Happy Mother's Day . . . or in June, Happy Father's Day . . . or in July, Happy . . . oh well, I think you get the picture.)

So, Happy Whatever, and we'll catch all you Buckoes and Buckettes a little later.

218